EMMA FROST MYSTERY - BOOK 4

CROSS YOUR HEART AND HOPE TO DIE

WILLOW ROSE

BOOKS BY THE AUTHOR

HARRY HUNTER MYSTERY SERIES

- ALL THE GOOD GIRLS
- RUN GIRL RUN
- NO OTHER WAY
- NEVER WALK ALONE

MARY MILLS MYSTERY SERIES

- WHAT HURTS THE MOST
- YOU CAN RUN
- YOU CAN'T HIDE
- CAREFUL LITTLE EYES

EVA RAE THOMAS MYSTERY SERIES

- DON'T LIE TO ME
- WHAT YOU DID
- NEVER EVER
- SAY YOU LOVE ME
- LET ME GO
- IT'S NOT OVER
- NOT DEAD YET
- TO DIE FOR

EMMA FROST SERIES

- ITSY BITSY SPIDER
- MISS DOLLY HAD A DOLLY

- Run, Run as Fast as You Can
- Cross Your Heart and Hope to Die
- Peek-a-Boo I See You
- Tweedledum and Tweedledee
- Easy as One, Two, Three
- There's No Place like Home
- Slenderman
- Where the Wild Roses Grow
- Waltzing Mathilda
- Drip Drop Dead
- Black Frost

JACK RYDER SERIES

- Hit the Road Jack
- Slip out the Back Jack
- The House that Jack Built
- Black Jack
- Girl Next Door
- Her Final Word
- Don't Tell

REBEKKA FRANCK SERIES

- One, Two...He is Coming for You
- Three, Four...Better Lock Your Door
- Five, Six...Grab your Crucifix
- Seven, Eight...Gonna Stay up Late
- Nine, Ten...Never Sleep Again
- Eleven, Twelve...Dig and Delve
- Thirteen, Fourteen...Little Boy Unseen
- Better Not Cry
- Ten Little Girls
- It Ends Here

MYSTERY/THRILLER/HORROR NOVELS

- Sorry Can't Save You
- In One Fell Swoop
- Umbrella Man
- Blackbird Fly
- To Hell in a Handbasket
- Edwina

HORROR SHORT-STORIES

- Mommy Dearest
- The Bird
- Better watch out
- Eenie, Meenie
- Rock-a-Bye Baby
- Nibble, Nibble, Crunch
- Humpty Dumpty
- Chain Letter

PARANORMAL SUSPENSE/ROMANCE NOVELS

- In Cold Blood
- The Surge
- Girl Divided

THE VAMPIRES OF SHADOW HILLS SERIES

- Flesh and Blood
- Blood and Fire
- Fire and Beauty
- Beauty and Beasts
- Beasts and Magic
- Magic and Witchcraft

- WITCHCRAFT AND WAR
- WAR AND ORDER
- ORDER AND CHAOS
- CHAOS AND COURAGE

THE AFTERLIFE SERIES

- BEYOND
- SERENITY
- ENDURANCE
- COURAGEOUS

THE WOLFBOY CHRONICLES

- A GYPSY SONG
- I AM WOLF

DAUGHTERS OF THE JAGUAR

- SAVAGE
- BROKEN

Cross my heart and hope to die
stick a needle in my eye
wait a moment, I spoke a lie
I never really wanted to die.
But if I may and if I might
my heart is open for tonight
though my lips are sealed
and a promise is true
I won't break my word
my word to you.

Cross my heart hope to die
stick a needle in my eye.
A secret's a secret my word is forever
I will tell no one about your cruel endeavor.
You claim no pain but I see right through
your words in everything you do.
Teary eyes broken heart
life has torn you apart

Cross my heart hope to die
stick a needle in my eye
I loved you then I love you now
I'll still love you though I'll break my vow.
I can't hold this secret any longer
it's hurting you not making you stronger.
You're my friend so I'll risk your respect
by hurting you I can protect
I'll save yourself since you will not
you might hate me but I'll give it a shot.
I'm willing to risk our bond that we own
so long as you're safe you won't be alone.

Cross my heart hope to die
   stick a needle in my eye
   break my promise
   tell a lie
   save my friend
   though, maybe it's "bye."

RELIGIOUS OATH IN THE EARLY 1900S

PROLOGUE
JULY 2005

HE WAS KEEPING a secret of the kind that could eat you up from the inside like a fire eats its way through a forest. But still, no one at the office could tell by looking at him. Definitely not today when he was smiling from ear to ear and his secretary had planted a glass of champagne in his hand that he now lifted into the air.

"To Nycom.com," he said with cheer.

"To Nycom.com," his employees answered.

They toasted and drank. Erik Gundtofte looked at his people with satisfaction while they mingled and chitchatted with laughter and happy faces. Yes, it was indeed a good day. The best day of Erik's young life. At the age of only twenty-five, his Internet company had just been sold for fifty million dollars to an American company. When investors were paid and bonuses were given, he would leave with around thirty million to himself. Enough for him to retire and enjoy his life with his beloved wife Maria and their two young children.

It was going to be a good life. They had already made their plans. They would start out by traveling around the globe for a year. They had discussed it for months, ever since Nycom.com contacted Erik and told him they had an offer he couldn't resist. They had put pins on a map and discussed it for weeks in a row. They talked about buying a boat and sailing around the world. They discussed trekking, and going by old trains. But they ended up deciding to do it the first class way ... to travel by air and live in nice hotels. Maria was the one who mostly wanted that, while Erik thought it could be great to backpack and stay in hostels.

"We have children, Erik," Maria had ended up saying. "We can't live with students in a greasy hostel. It would have worked when we were nineteen, but we're not anymore. We have little ones to consider."

So they agreed on doing it the expensive way. Lord knew they could afford it. It was a new way of living that Erik had to get used to. To never want for anything again. To never worry about how to pay the bills again. It was almost overwhelming.

Both he and Maria knew which countries they were dying to visit and now it was all finally about to become a reality.

Erik couldn't stop smiling. He had all his stuff packed in a box on his desk and once he left the office this very afternoon, he was never coming back.

"So what are you planning on doing with the rest of your life?" his friend Jacob, who had worked for him ever since the beginning in 1999, asked.

Erik shrugged. "Travel. Enjoy my family. Maybe write a book or do some conferences where I tell people how I made my fortune. Lay low, seize the day, move to the Caribbean, who knows?" Erik said laughing.

"The world really is your oyster, huh?" said Jacob.

Erik nodded while drinking. "Yup. There is nothing I can't do. I'm free to go wherever I want to go, free to do and buy whatever I want to, whatever I dream of. As long as I don't go berserk, the money should last for the rest of my life."

"It certainly is enough. You should be very proud of yourself," Jacob said.

"Well the deal is good for all of us," Erik said. "You're leaving with some seven million dollars yourself as far as I recall."

Jacob smiled and nodded. "I most certainly am. I can't deny that."

Erik studied the face of his old friend and companion. They had known each other for so many years and shared so many ups and downs together. It had been a rollercoaster and Erik was glad it was over.

Jacob was scrutinizing Erik's face. Erik noticed and smiled awkwardly. He sipped from his glass. He never did like champagne too much. Not the real expensive kind. It was too sour. His wife always said he was never going to make a good member of high class society. Erik didn't mind that.

"You got so serious all of a sudden," Jacob said. "You're not having second thoughts, are you?"

Erik forced a smile again. "About the sale? No, no of course not. This is the best for everybody."

"That's not what I meant and you know it," Jacob replied seriously.

Erik avoided his friend's eyes. They both knew perfectly well what he was talking about. It had been on Erik's mind a lot lately. It tore at him and made it hard to really enjoy this day. He couldn't tell Jacob, but he had started to doubt if he was ever going to be able to be really happy, to enjoy this money and his freedom fully if he had to carry this secret around with him. It just didn't feel right. When he was working day and night to build the company, he had been able to not think about it, to displace it, but he wasn't certain he could do that anymore. Years had gone by since it happened and keeping it hidden inside was getting harder and harder for him. And he was afraid that Jacob could tell. That was the worst part. Erik knew he couldn't hide his growing doubts from his oldest friend.

Jacob grabbed his arm and pulled him aside. "You know you can't tell."

Erik sighed and sipped his champagne. He didn't say anything, but he was considering it. Now that everything was done with the sale, there really was no excuse not to anymore. He knew he wasn't going to be able to live with this secret eating at him from the inside. But he also knew that telling might ruin everything for him. But which was worse? Living with this, having it eating at him for the rest of his life or spending a few years in jail and having told the truth? Should he maybe wait till the kids were older? No, he had to make things right. He had to tell.

"You have sworn an oath, Erik," Jacob continued.

"I know," Erik said, thinking of the consequences. "But it is eating me alive, you know?"

"Swallow it up like the rest of us. It'll get easier with age. Think about the money and the life you're about to have. You can't say anything. Do you hear me? You just can't."

"I don't know if I can live with myself like this," Erik said.

Jacob stared at him with furor. He grabbed his collar and pulled Erik close till they were face to face. "Don't do it, Erik. I swear I'll ..."

Erik breathed heavily. "You'll what Jacob?"

Jacob let go of Erik's collar. He shook his head. "Why now? Where is all this coming from all of a sudden? So many years have passed and it never seemed to bother you before. Why now?"

Erik shrugged. "I don't know. I just can't stop thinking about it. It keeps me awake at night. It won't be long before Maria starts asking questions. She can sense these things, Jacob. She knows when something is going on with me. It's like an avalanche. Once it starts rolling, it never stops. I can't stop it."

"Well, you have to. It's for your own sake too, you know. If this gets out, we're all going down. Including you. You'll lose everything. Do you hear me? Everything you've worked for the last several years."

Erik exhaled. Jacob had hit the nail on the head.

"I know. I know," Erik said.

"So you're not going to say anything?" Jacob asked, scrutinizing Erik's face once again.

Erik scoffed. "Of course not."

"Cross your heart and hope to die?"

"Cross my heart and hope to die."

1

DECEMBER 2013

I HAD RESERVED a window seat for the long train ride. I found it and sat down. Maya and Victor were standing outside on the platform with my dad and Morten. They had brought me to the train station in Esbjerg on the mainland. It was a long trip for them and I told them they didn't have to do it, but they decided to make a day of it. They were going to go Christmas shopping in the city for the rest of the day before heading back to the island.

I smiled and waved at them feeling a pinch in my heart. I hated to leave all of them, even though it was only for the weekend. I loathed myself for getting all mushy; it often happened to me in December and around Christmas, but I felt like crying, looking at all my loved ones. The second the train started moving, I regretted my plans, but it was too late. I waved like crazy and pressed my nose against the window until I couldn't see them any longer. Then I sighed and leaned back in the soft chair of the first-class carriage. I wasn't alone. Three men in suits were looking business-like, talking on the phone, reading the papers and working on their laptops. I preferred staring out the window looking at the landscape passing by, which was covered in a thin layer of white snow. It was beautiful. I sighed and looked at the man sitting in front of me working on his computer looking like everything he did was very important.

"I'm going to Skagen," I said.

The man looked up from the screen and stared at me as if he was wondering if I was retarded or just plain annoying. In Denmark, people never spoke to strangers on public transportation or anywhere else, if they could avoid it. My theory was that it had something to do with the cold. The cold made people grumpy. I didn't care that he thought I was crazy. I was happy and looking forward to this weekend away. No grumpy old man was going to change that.

"Going to stay at Brinkloev Badehotel," I continued.

The man's face lit up. I knew it would. That was why I was so eager to tell him. It was one of the most expensive hotels in the country. It was located in Skagen, the northernmost town in Denmark, *the top of Denmark*, in the dunes with views directly over Vesterhavet. I had read all about it on the Internet while checking out my old class-mates' Facebook profiles as well, so I would know how they had done for themselves.

"That is a very nice place," the man said politely. "You'll have a great vacation up there." Then he looked back down at his screen again, probably hoping I would keep quiet for the rest of the way.

"I know," I said. "Going there to my high school reunion. I am so excited to see how many of the old friends will show up. It will be fun to catch up and see what people have been up to. The things we don't already know from Facebook, that is," I chuckled.

The man smiled politely, then returned to his screen.

Typical of the boring Danes, I thought to myself. *Never want to talk, always busy. He's probably just watching porn on that thing.* The thought made me laugh. The man raised his eyebrows and looked at me again.

"Sorry," I said. "Just thought about something funny."

"I see," the man said.

I tapped my fingers on the table and looked out the window while my stomach growled. I rose to my feet and looked down the aisle through the train. I spotted the lady with the food wagon further down. In first class, the breakfast was free. I watched her as she pushed the wagon closer and sat down as soon as she entered through the sliding doors. She was dressed like a flight attendant and smiled like one as she spoke.

"Breakfast roll?"

"Yes please, two please," I said. "And coffee please. And butter, and cheese and ... uh ... jam. And a chocolate bar please. Do you have hot chocolate?"

The lady looked at me, puzzled, then smiled again. "Sure." She pulled out the food and placed it in front of me. Then she poured hot chocolate in a cup.

"Do you have whipped cream?" I asked.

"No. I'm sorry. I don't."

"Okay," I said disappointed and looked at the food in front of me. I couldn't wait to get started.

The man lifted his eyes from the screen just enough to make me feel bad about all the food. I shook my head while buttering the roll and putting cheese on top of it.

"And for you, sir?" she asked the man behind the laptop.

I bit down on my roll with butter, cheese and jam on top. Just the way I preferred it. It was still warm and the butter had melted. I sipped my hot chocolate with my eyes closed. It was perfect for a cold winter day.

"Just a cup of coffee," the man said.

"Sugar? Milk?" The attendant asked with her high-pitched, forced-polite voice.

The man in the grey suit shook his head with his grey hair and a look to his eyes like it was the most despicable thing he had ever heard of.

The woman pushed the wagon past our seats without saying anything more. I ate and drank greedily. I had been up early this morning to take the ferry to the mainland. I was hungry and no looks from an old grey man were going to make me feel bad about it.

While I ate, I took out my iPad and looked at the e-mail I had received inviting me to this reunion. I was wondering who it was that had actually sent us the e-mail, since it wasn't signed by anyone, just by *The party-committee of the class of '98*. It was a little odd, I thought, that they wanted to keep it a secret who was behind the gathering, but maybe it was supposed to be a surprise of some sort. At least I was about to find out.

I was just happy that someone had actually taken the time to arrange all this for us. It was the first time we would get together since we graduated nearly fifteen years ago. Fifteen years?

Had it really been that long?

I looked at the e-mail. It was strange that someone chose to have us reunited this year of all years. Why now?

Maybe it wasn't important. The important part was that we got to see each other again and have some great food and spend the weekend in a beautiful, luxurious hotel.

I, for one, couldn't wait.

2

DECEMBER 2013

HE HAD TAKEN in an acute patient even though it was Saturday morning and even though he was in a hurry. The poor patient was in serious pain and needed his assistance. Preben Krogh wasn't the type of dentist who would say no to a patient in distress. Especially not when he was being paid double because it was the weekend.

The patient was now in the chair, bent backwards and moaning in pain as Preben asked him to open his mouth. He looked inside it and found the problem immediately. A big brown round hole in one of the patient's back teeth.

Preben sighed and found his instruments. "We need to fix this right away," he said as he looked at his watch. It was only eight in the morning. He could still make it to Skagen before lunch if he took the car. He lived in Aarhus and it was only a couple of hours away. If only he could get this hole filled quickly. If only this patient would lie still in the chair.

"Please, try not to move," he said when the patient squirmed.

"I'm trying," the patient said, muffled.

"It might hurt a little," Preben said and started scraping off some of the dirt that had gathered around the hole.

The patient whimpered. He was breaking out in a sweat on his forehead and upper lip. He had once told Preben that he was absolutely terrified of going to the dentist. That was why he never went unless it was an emergency.

Why ... I have never ... the imbecile didn't even care enough to brush his teeth before he got here this morning.

It was the third time in the last three months that this same patient had called with an acute problem like this. It was kind of getting on Preben's nerves a little. It was about time someone taught him a lesson.

"I told you to stay off the sweets," Preben said, annoyed.

The patient spoke while Preben had his hands inside his mouth and Preben didn't understand a single word and didn't care to either. It was probably just more excuses. Stupid excuses for why he was still eating that stuff, why he didn't brush his teeth properly, and so on and so on. It sickened Preben to have to listen to all these stupid excuses. The fact was, the patient, and many other patients, was simply too freaking LAZY to take proper care of his teeth. What was it about dental hygiene that was so difficult? It was hardly rocket science, for crying out loud. It was so incredibly simple it almost hurt. Simply brush your teeth three times a day, or even just twice a day would do, and floss. Floss, floss, floss. That was it. There really wasn't any more to it than that. Why wouldn't people listen? Preben was so sick of it, so sick of people not listening to his advice.

"Maybe if you came in for a check-up once in a while, we wouldn't have these emergencies," he said.

The patient squirmed in the chair again as Preben found the drill. "Aren't you going to sedate me first?" the patient asked. "You usually do."

Preben smiled and started the drill. It made a loud sound and the patient shrieked. Preben laughed.

"Not this time."

Then he held the patient down while drilling his tooth out, letting him scream as loud as he wanted to. It was, after all, Saturday and they were alone in the clinic. No one would be able to hear him.

"Do try and lie still. It would make this so much easier on the both of us. Now, the whole reason I have to drill this hole is that it is actually filled with decayed tooth material and the bacteria that caused the decay in the first place," Preben yelled, trying to drown out the noise from the drill and the patient's screams. "In order to correctly prepare the tooth for a filling, I must remove this decayed material. Then I can fill in the clean hole with an amalgam filling."

Preben felt drops of sweat on his forehead as he drilled the hole and held the whimpering patient down in the chair. When he was done, he stopped the drill and pulled it out. The patient looked at him in distress.

"What the hell are you doing?" he yelled and got up from the chair while holding a hand to his cheek. "That hurt like hell."

Preben looked at the young man. He had never really noticed his face before now or that big nose of his. That was how it often was when you spent most of your time looking inside your patients' mouths. Then he smiled.

"That was kind of the idea," he said.

The patient looked angry.

Oh my, Preben thought to himself. *A little upset are we?*

"Why? Why would you drill without sedation?" the patient asked.

Preben sighed. "I'll tell you why, my friend. Because I want you to remember how painful it was the next time you want to eat some of those sugary sweets that I have told you OVER and OVER again not to eat. I want you to remember how badly it hurt the NEXT time you decide to skip the brushing or won't bother to floss because it's boring or whatever your little excuse might be. I want you to always remember the pain that you felt here today so I won't have to rush down here every third month because you have another emergency that simply can't WAIT. Do you read me?"

The young man stared at Preben for a long time. He was still holding a hand to his cheek.

"Do you understand?" Preben repeated harshly.

The patient whimpered, then nodded. "Yes."

"Yes, sir," Preben corrected him.

"Yes, sir."

"Now get back in that chair and let me put in the filling. I have some-where more important to be later today."

3

DECEMBER 2013

"WHAT I DON'T UNDERSTAND IS how this could have happened? I thought you were on the pill?"

Bo looked at Line. She avoided his eyes and continued packing her suitcase. She was determined not to let his words get to her. She was happy and wanted to remain that way. They had been arguing all night and now she was running late. She was also getting really tired of discussing this. He kept asking her the same questions over and over again.

She shrugged. "Well I don't know, Bo. I guess you can't depend on them a hundred percent."

Line found her long jacket and put it on the bed. She would wear it since the weatherman on TV this morning said it was going to get cold. And windy since a possible storm was heading towards Denmark from Norway. Line needed the jacket to protect her stomach and the baby from getting cold. It was time for her to start thinking differently. It wasn't just about her anymore. She had a responsibility.

Bo slammed his fist onto the table. "God dammit, Line. We just met each other a month ago."

"I know sweetie, but that's just the way it is."

"How are you not more upset about this?" he asked.

Line looked at him and tilted her head. Poor Bo. Poor very young Bo who had been taken completely aback by the fact that Line had become pregnant. She tried hard to hide her joy, since for her this was a long awaited event. And for her mother as well. Actually, her mother had been the one who came up with the idea. Line was her only chance of ever getting a grandchild and when she saw that chance getting smaller every day that passed, she decided to give Line a piece of advice.

"Go out, find some guy, any guy, and get yourself pregnant. It's the only way for you. Your clock is ticking."

Line smiled to herself and closed the suitcase. Her mom was right. At the age of thirty-three, it was about time. She didn't really care if Bo wanted to be a part of it or not. After all, he was only twenty-one and worked as a bartender downtown in Jomfru Ane Gade in the heart of Aalborg. He was used to picking up women and never seeing them again. Line had kept coming to him, picking him up after his shift was over and dragging him home with her, with the sole purpose of him donating his sperm.

"I guess I'm just ready for this," she said.

"Well I'm not. I ... I ..." Bo moaned and covered his face with his hands. "I can't have a child. You must get an abortion."

Line laughed and threw back her head. "Oh Bo. You're such a kid."

"I mean it goddammit," he said and slammed his fist on the table again. "I can't have a child."

She shrugged. "Well too bad for you then. I'm having it anyway."

Bo looked at her and moaned. "How? How can you be so indifferent? I don't understand. Do you really want to destroy my life?"

"You don't have to be a part of it. I'm perfectly capable of doing this on my own," Line said and packed her toothbrush. "I'm just telling you about it because you deserve to know. That's all. And, plus, I need the money."

"What money?"

"To raise our child. It's not cheap you know. You'll have to pay child support. Those are the rules, Bo. Don't you know that?"

He looked baffled. "But ... but ..."

Line laughed again. "Oh, Bo. There is just so much you don't know, isn't there? Well, this will teach you to be more careful in the future. Now if you'll excuse me, I have to catch a train."

She closed her suitcase and pulled it down from the bed. It was heavier than anticipated. Maybe she had packed too many clothes, after all. Well, she needed a lot to choose from. It was important that she looked her best at this event. She wanted to dazzle all the others with how young and beautiful she still was. And even better, she now also had the glow of a pregnant woman.

"Where are you going anyway?" asked Bo tiredly.

"I have a high school reunion in Skagen to attend. And I'm very much looking forward to seeing everybody and telling them the great news."

"What great news?"

"That I'm not a failure after all, like they all assumed I would be. I'm expecting a child and will start a family soon."

Bo exhaled deeply. "Was that was this was all about? You wanted to get pregnant before your high school reunion so you could show them?"

Line's smile froze. "Well, when you put it like that, it sounds awful. You must understand that I don't have many other things going for me right now. Working full-time at a gas station is hardly a story of success. At least I'll have this."

Bo looked like he could punch her. "You're sick, do you know that?"

Line shrugged with a wide, slightly maniacal smile. "So be it. Now scram. I have a train to catch."

4

DECEMBER 2013

"THEY WANT to take you in for more questioning, Soren," the lawyer said on the phone. "Probably will come for you on Monday or Tuesday."

Soren Hedelund closed his eyes. "I already told them I didn't do it when they had me in earlier today. It's all just lies on her part. I don't want to have to keep telling them the same things over and over again. She's making it all up." He heard the desperation in his own voice and was certain the lawyer heard it too.

"Well, I believe you, but they take these matters very seriously, Soren. It's a big deal," the lawyer said. Then he paused and sighed. "You might want to tell your wife at some point."

"Margit? Why? Why on earth would I do that?"

"Because she will find out sooner or later. It's already in the papers this morning. They don't know your name yet, but the story is out there, Soren. She might hear it from a neighbor or one of your co-workers or someone at the hospital. This is a small town. People talk."

Soren sighed and looked through the window at his wife who was cooking him breakfast in the kitchen. She smiled when their eyes met. He smiled back and pretended that whatever he was talking about on the phone wasn't important. Then he turned his head and looked at the city in front of him. He had walked out on the balcony to take the call so she wouldn't hear anything. Margit didn't need to know. No, he was determined to spare her from these horrifying accusations against him. It would just upset her and that wasn't good for her in her condition.

"I can't do it. The doctor told me not to upset her. She has too much on her plate as it is and has to focus on her treatment and all. I can't let this distract her from getting better. I simply can't," he said.

"I know it must be hard with the chemo treatments and all, but I still think you should tell her, Soren. It's going to be big. You might have to leave your job," the lawyer said.

Soren's heart stopped. *Leave my job?*

"But ... but ... they can't ... don't they know she's lying?"

"A seventeen year old girl was raped, for crying out loud," the lawyer yelled. "She was in your care at the time."

"But ... but surely they don't think ... they think I did it, don't they?"

"Well you were alone with her in the ambulance at the time. She claims you sedated her and raped her on the way to the hospital."

"But she was so drunk she couldn't even walk, how can anyone take what she says seriously?"

"You're a paramedic, Soren. You have a responsibility, do I have to explain what that means? If the tests prove she is right, then you're done. You'll never work as a paramedic again. You'll go to jail. We're looking at at least two years here. I might be able to get it down to fourteen months."

Soren sighed and leaned against the railing. He looked down, wondering if he would die on the spot if he jumped now. Then he turned his head and looked at his wife. She gave him another of her rare smiles. He couldn't leave her like that. What about the kids? If she died, they would be all alone. He couldn't lose his job either. Who would support her? Who would support the children? Soren closed his eyes. How could he have been so stupid? How could he have been so careless? Usually, when they picked up young girls at parties, they were passed out or at least too drunk to feel anything. This girl had been conscious, but he had done it anyway. Why? Because she was irresistible. She had wanted it too, he was certain she did. The way she moaned and smiled on the bed when he had strapped her down. He had given her a sedative alright, but maybe he had been too fast. Maybe he had acted before the sedative kicked in properly. He didn't know, but something had gone terribly wrong. The girl had told the nurses at the hospital and now they were all on his case. It had been on the front page of the *Zeeland Times* this morning. Some reporter named Rebekka Franck knew it was him and kept calling him on his phone. How she had found out his name, he didn't know, but the lawyer was right. It wasn't going to be long before Margit found out and all hell broke loose.

"I might tell her when I get back," Soren said.

"Where are you going?" the lawyer asked.

"To Skagen. I have a high school reunion this weekend. I'm leaving by train in an hour."

"This is very bad timing, Soren," the lawyer said.

"I know. But I'll be back Monday and then I'll be all over this, okay? I think getting away will help clear my head a little."

The lawyer sighed deeply. "Okay then. I'll talk to you Monday. Remember don't talk to any journalists, okay?"

"Got it."

"And one final thing."

"What's that?"

"Did you do it? Did you rape that girl?"

Soren hesitated. He stared at his wife while thoughts lined up in his mind. Should he tell him? Should he come clean, maybe say the girl told him she wanted to have sex with him in the back of the ambulance? No, No. They would fire him on the spot. He loved his job. But weren't they going to fire him anyway? A story like this didn't just disappear, did it? It lingered with a person, didn't it? There was always going to be that doubt wasn't there?

"Of course not," he said and closed his eyes.

"Are you sure?"

"Cross my heart and hope to die."

"Good. Talk to you on Monday."

"Bye."

Soren put the phone back in his pocket and went inside. He walked towards her, then grabbed her by the shoulders and kissed her.

"Wow, what was that for?"

"Just to show you how much I love you."

She smiled. Her eyes looked so dark. He could see her cheekbones very clearly. She felt so small, so fragile between his hands. He stared at her throat. He could see the veins through the pale skin. It would be so easy to put an end to her suffering right here and now. He might even be able to strangle her using just one hand. Then it would be all over. He could then jump from the balcony.

Soren breathed heavily while he stared at his wife's throat. Everything around him went quiet. All he could hear was the sound of the blood rushing through his veins. A small voice came up behind them and made him change his mind.

"Mommy, I need your help."

Soren let go of Margit and she attended their daughter who had gotten her brush stuck in the back of her hair. Soren closed his eyes and breathed to calm himself down. His heart was still racing in his chest.

"Can you believe this?" his wife said after she was done and their daughter had left the kitchen.

Soren opened his eyes and forced a gentle smile. "What's that dear?"

She held up the paper with the story on the front cover.

GIRL RAPED IN AMBULANCE.

Soren stared at it with a wildly beating heart. He had meant to remove the paper and throw it out, but then the lawyer had called at that instant and he had forgotten all about it.

"Do you think it is someone you know who did this?" asked Margit. "Oh my God. It says here it was someone from your station. Roskilde Falck-station. Oh my God, Soren who do you think it could be? Ah, I bet it is Bent. He always looks at me so weirdly. He is creepy. I bet it's him. Don't you?"

Soren bit his lip, once again imagining killing her. Embarrassed that she might see it on his face, he looked down and shrugged.

"I don't know," he said and looked at his watch. "It could be anybody.

Anyway, I have to get going now." He turned and stormed inside the bedroom where he grabbed his suitcase and jacket.

"Don't you want breakfast first?" Margit asked when he returned.

"I'll eat on the way. They have food on the train. Good bye now."

"But ..."

He leaned over and kissed her on the cheek, then stormed out of the apartment and down the stairs. When he reached the street below, he was panting and his heart was racing like crazy. As he walked towards the train station with the suitcase in his hand, he had only one unbearable thought in his mind.

If I stayed one more minute, I would probably have killed her.

5

DECEMBER 2013

JACOB LOMHOLDT DIDN'T PARTICULARLY like Christmas or any other holiday for that matter. It was all just a load of crap meant for you to spend money and for the workers in his company to get lazy, have stupid parties, and not focus on work.

Christmas was also the time of year when he was reminded yet again, that he was alone. That he didn't have anyone in his life. When all the workers at his investment company went home to be with their families for the holidays, he could look forward to spending yet another vacation alone in his mansion by the ocean in Hellerup.

At least there were still a couple of weeks till Christmas and, even though December had arrived, he still didn't see it as any excuse to become sloppy. As usual, he would tolerate no chitchatting by the water cooler, or anyone talking privately on the phone and certainly not someone checking Facebook on their computer. Jacob monitored all his worker's movements and whereabouts on the Internet. He read their e-mails and made sure they didn't spend their time doing anything other than make sure he became richer. It hadn't made him more popular, but it certainly had made him and his company successful. He knew what they called him behind his back, but he didn't care. All he had ever wanted in his life was to get rich. And that he had succeeded at.

Now he was standing in his bedroom with views over Oresund and could see the coast of Sweden on the other side. He was naked and smoking a cigarette while the cleaning lady whom he had just had sex with was getting dressed behind him.

"Now get out," he growled, once he saw she was halfway decent.

The small Asian girl bowed humbly. "Yes, Mr. Lomholdt."

He growled again and she left. She had been with him the last month or so, but he was getting bored with her. She didn't please him any longer and he was going to have her replaced with someone else next week. He would call the agency on Monday.

Jacob sighed and smoked his cigarette. He looked at his packed suitcase in the corner and wondered why he was even bothering to go.

A high school reunion. What could be more ridiculous?

Yet there was still a part of him that was intrigued to go. He hadn't quite figured out just yet why that was. Maybe it was just the thought of seeing all those bastards from back then and rubbing his success in their faces. Yes, that was probably it. He would take the limo and really rub it in. Wear the most expensive of his suits. Show off. Make them sick with envy.

He looked at his own reflection in the full-sized mirror at the end of the bedroom.

"Mr. Lomholdt," he said.

He liked to call himself that. Just like he always made the women he slept with call him that. It made him feel important. Like he was somebody. Which he actually was. He was *a somebody*. Not just anybody.

Anyone can shoot out a couple of kids, marry some idiot, and have a family. What you've done, Mr. Lomholdt, is extraordinary. It's unique and they'll see it right away. You'll make them feel small and insignificant.

Jacob laughed out loud while looking at his well-muscled body which he had spent many hours shaping at his private gym on his estate north of Copenhagen. In school he had always been a small guy, but many years of bodybuilding had given him a body many envied. He was muscular and the women liked that. They liked him to be the strong one in bed, they liked him to be in charge. The only thing that bothered him right now was a small pain in the lower part of his back. It had arrived last night and had still been there this morning. It had even made it difficult for him to perform properly with the small Asian girl. It annoyed him.

Jacob turned his body and looked at his back in the mirror. No, there was nothing to see. Maybe he had just strained a muscle during his workout the day before. That was probably it.

Looking at what he had accomplished with his body filled him with pride.

Yes, they were all going to look at him with great envy and desire. That was worth the long trip to the other end of the country. It was worth it just to see it in their eyes.

Jacob found his most expensive suit and packed it for the dinner, then found another Armani suit and put it on for the arrival. He was going to look his best. Make the girls want him and the guys want to be him.

He called the chauffeur and told him to get ready to leave in a few minutes, then hung up and stared at his own reflection one last time. Jacob fixed a small straw of hair.

"There you go. Perfection," he told himself. "Now go up there and dazzle them. Make them want what you have."

6

JULY 2005

ERIK WOKE UP HAPPY. Maria was lying next to him and he could hear his two daughters playing in their room in the small apartment in Copenhagen. Maria was still asleep and he looked at her while relishing the moment.

This is it. It doesn't get much better than this. At this moment I have everything.

He turned his head and looked around at the small bedroom that had been theirs for nearly four years now. That was all about to change. Now they would enter a new phase in their lives. It was about time they said goodbye to their old life.

Today marks a new beginning.

The apartment had served them well, though. It was in one of the poorer neighborhoods just outside of town with lots of crime. It was small. Tiny even ... and way too small for a family of four. But it had been cheap at the time and that was what they needed when he started up the company. To have as few expenses as possible. They hadn't planned to have children already, but Maria had gotten pregnant by accident soon after they met and, as it turned out, it was twins.

So here he was. At the age of twenty-five, Erik was a husband, a father

of two and a millionaire. He sighed and seized the moment. This was what
he had dreamt of. This moment of peace and tranquility, when he knew
everything was going to be alright, when he had finally made it big.

No it wasn't going to get much better than this. Now it was time for
them to enjoy what they had accomplished. The world was open to them
now and they could do anything. Anything!

They could go to Disneyworld today if they wanted to. They could buy
a huge TV or the biggest teddy bear in the toy store down at the mall. Yes,
Erik would finally get to spoil his kids and his wife the way they all
deserved and he could finally enjoy the many years of hard work he had
put into building his company. This was what everybody dreamed of. To
have the freedom to do what they pleased. And it was all his to enjoy.

If only ...

Erik sighed again and looked at his beloved wife. The girls were fighting
about something in the room next door. It wouldn't be long until they came in
crying and screaming. Erik smiled and stroked his wife gently across her hair.

*Why can't you just let it go, Erik? No one will ever know if you don't tell.
No one needs to know.*

He heard feet in the hallway and soon the door to the bedroom opened.
Both girls entered with tears in their eyes.

"Mooom?" Isabella said.

"Mooom?" Nanna said. "Bella is being mean."

Maria opened her eyes slowly and looked at the two girls. "I'll be right
there, she said with a tired voice. She had been through so much the last
few years. While he had built the company, she had taken care of everything at home. Now it was his turn to help her out. She deserved it.

"Let me take care of it," Erik said and kissed her.

Then he jumped out of bed and pretended to be a huge monster. "Here
comes the tickling monster!" he yelled.

The girls screamed loudly and ran out the door followed by Erik who
was making grumbling and growling sounds, trying to sound like Sully from
Monsters Inc.

The girls hid in their room and Erik ran after them, grabbed them both and tickled them till they screamed for him to stop. When they had enough and they continued their play, Erik jumped back into bed with his wife and kissed her soft neck, smelled her hair, and lay close to her for as long as he could before they were interrupted once again.

It was Isabella. "Moom?"

"Yes sweetie?" Erik said and looked at her to let her know he was taking care of things this morning.

"There is someone at the door."

"I'll be right there."

Erik found his pants and a shirt and walked to the front door. Outside stood the neighbor. She looked upset.

"Yes? Mrs. Rasmussen? What's wrong?" Asked Erik. "Are you alright? Has something happened?"

"I ... I think your car is on fire. Yours is the old black Toyota, right? I just looked out the window and saw a big fire down in the parking lot. I'm pretty sure it is your car. I called the fire department."

"What is it, Daddy?" asked Isabella behind Erik's back.

"Stay here with mommy," he said and stormed down the stairs of the apartment complex.

He ran out into the parking lot where he saw a huge pillar of fire reaching straight into the air from the spot where he had parked the car the day before. Erik stopped and stared at his old car, his old companion through the last four years, as it was devoured by the greedy flames.

Erik heard a shriek behind him and turned to see Isabella who had followed him down the stairs.

"Daddy! Is that our car?"

He grabbed her in his arms and lifted her up. "Yes, sweetie. It's okay."

In the distance he could hear the wailing sirens from the approaching fire trucks.

"Daddy! Our car!" Isabella continued. "Buddy is in there."

Erik stared at his daughter. Buddy was her favorite teddy-bear. "Buddy was in the car?"

Isabella was crying loudly now. "Yes, I forgot him in there yesterday."

Erik pulled his daughter closer and held her tight. "I'm afraid Buddy is gone now. But you know what?"

Isabella sniffled. "No?"

"Daddy will buy you a new and much better one. I promise, alright? Maybe a Build-A-Bear like you always wanted. What do you say to that?"

"But ... but they're too expensive. You always say that."

"Not anymore, sweetheart. From now on, we can afford it."

"We have money now?"

Erik laughed. "We have lots of money, sweetheart."

She sniffled again. He wiped her eyes.

"So we can buy a new car too?" she asked.

"We can get a brand new car," he said.

The fire trucks entered the parking lot flanked by a police car. There was a lot of yelling as the firefighters pulled out the hoses and started spurting water on the remains of the car. The police spoke to Erik and neighbors gathered to watch the scene. Maria and Nanna came down as well, but went back up to the apartment after a few minutes since Nanna thought it was *too scary*.

"So when will we get the new car, Daddy?" asked Isabella when they had finally put out the fire and there was nothing left but a small black bundle on the asphalt. It felt symbolic, really. In some way, it marked the ending of their lives as poor people.

Erik turned around and started walking back to the apartment. "Today, Bella. Let's do it today. What color would you like it to be?"

7

DECEMBER 2013

I TOOK a taxi from the station to the hotel. The driver was the chatty type who never stopped talking as we drove out of the small town. I watched with joy as the old houses passed my window. They were so beautifully painted in the yellow that was so distinctive to Skagen.

The town was literally situated at the tip of the country and had water on each side of it. It was a peninsula and it marked the end of Denmark. On the other side of the ocean were Sweden and Norway. I had been to Skagen once before as a child, but other than that, the place had always been a mystery to me. It was known to be Denmark's main fishing port and also had a thriving tourist industry, attracting some two million people annually. It was also known to have attracted a lot of artists, the so-called Skagen-painters which was a group of Scandinavian artists who visited the area every summer from the late 1870s until the turn of the century. They were attracted by the scenery, the fishermen and the quality of light which encouraged them to paint *en plein air* following the example of the French Impressionists. I remember learning about them in school ... that they broke away from the rigid traditions of the Danish and Swedish art academies, preferring the modern trends they had experienced in Paris. In recent years, Skagen was also known as a place that attracted the younger part of the royal family who would summer there every now and then along with the jet-set of the country.

"So Brinkloev Badehotel, huh?" the driver asked curiously and looked at me in his rearview mirror. "That's a nice place to stay."

"I know," I said, knowing it was usually way out of my league financially, even if my three books were very successful.

We drove for fifteen minutes while the driver kept talking about how this time of year was very quiet up there and business was bad, since tourists came in the summer to see the light and visit the tip where you could actually stand in the sand and have two oceans, Kattegat and the North Sea, on each side of you. You could even see out into the water where the two oceans met. It was called *Grenen*, the branch.

I knew most of what he had told me and knew I had tried to stand there as a child, but I couldn't remember much about it. I nodded my interest and looked out the window as we drove through a huge plantation. Nothing but bushes and trees for a long stretch.

"It's a long way out," I said.

And a long way back.

The trees were large and dark. There was something very sinister about it. I shivered faintly.

"Brinkloev is located behind the plantation, in the dunes right out by the ocean. Very nice," the driver said.

I felt a tickling sensation in my stomach as we finally put the plantation behind us and I spotted a huge old building in the distance. I had seen pictures of the hotel on the Internet but none of them did it justice. It was gorgeous. Illuminated by the sun that was so rare at this time of year, I had my first glimpse of the hotel that seemed to stretch along the coast as far as I could see. It was an old building, made entirely from wood, looking very similar to an old farm, but it was beautifully maintained and had a modern touch to it with its hundreds of big windows facing the ocean. As the driver parked on the gravel outside, I looked at the building and hoped I would get one of those rooms under the roof with the windows facing the ocean.

"Enjoy your stay," the driver said as I paid him and got out of the car.

Two bell-boys in uniform came out and grabbed my suitcase. I thought it was a bit of overkill to have two of them with only my one small suitcase.

I went inside and approached the counter. A tall clerk looked at me with a smile. "Name please?"

I opened my mouth to speak, but someone beat me to it.

"Emma Frost!" a voice said behind me.

I turned my head and looked into the eyes of Jacob Lomholt wearing a very expensive suit. He looked great and as annoying as ever. I had never liked the guy and had kind of hoped he wouldn't show up. But there he was. Standing in front of me with a smirk, looking like he wanted me to comment on his appearance.

"Jacob," I said and gave him an awkward hug. "You look great."

"So, how have you been, Emma? You look great too. I haven't had time to read your books, unfortunately, but I hear they're doing well?"

I smiled. "Yes. They're doing pretty good. I can't complain. And you?"

"Oh, you don't want to hear about that," he said.

He had no idea how right he was. I knew he wanted me to ask more, but I didn't. I really didn't want to talk to him.

"Well it looks like you've done pretty well for yourself as well," I said and received my key from the clerk.

"To the right up the stairs and to your left," he said.

"Thanks," I said.

"I can't complain either," Jacob said with a smirk. He had always been a pompous bastard and growing up had only made it worse as far as I could tell.

"Well I'll find my room, then catch you later," I said hoping to get away from him.

"Sure," he said and received his key as well.

"Lunch is served at 12.30 in The Yellow Room as we call the smaller of our two restaurants," the clerk said.

"Guess I'll see you then," Jacob said.

"Guess so," I said, hoping I would be placed as far away from him as possible during lunch.

8

DECEMBER 2013

FINISHING the acute patient took longer than expected and Preben Krogh had to drive very fast in order to make it to Skagen before lunch. He didn't mind though. He enjoyed listening to the motor roar on his new BMW that he had bought just a month ago. Business had been good the last several years and he hardly ever spent any money on vacations and other stuff that drained your account. Instead, he liked to buy himself a muscle-car every now and then and see how fast it could go on the narrow Danish roads in the countryside.

The road in front of him was wide open. Not a car in sight. Nothing but hills and a few turns. Preben accelerated and listened to the sound of the engine. It was like music to his ears. Better than Bach or that stupid opera that his ex-wife loved so much.

They had been divorced for a year now and nothing pleased him more. He was sick of her and her mood swings. In the end, it had gotten so bad he never knew which version of her he would come home to. Her doctor told her she was depressed and had given her pills for it. Because she couldn't conceive a child. Preben understood why she was sad, but to be honest, he didn't take part in her grief. He was quite relieved when it turned out they couldn't have children. He had seen how those things had destroyed his friends' lives one after another. No, that wasn't for him. He wanted different things. He wanted to be able to play tennis when he wanted or golf instead of spending the weekend at loud birthday parties with annoying kids screaming his ear off.

But Lisbeth had wanted it differently. She had asked him if they could adopt, but he had refused.

"I don't want to have to take care of some one else's kid," he had told her. "It's out of the question."

After that, things had gone terribly wrong between the two of them. Lisbeth had cried herself to sleep every night and refused to have anything to do with him. She started calling him a *heartless bastard* and sometimes wouldn't even speak to him for days. After a couple of weeks, Preben had stopped caring. He was happy as long as he got to do what he wanted. It wasn't like he had even loved Lisbeth anyway. No, he had loved someone else for most of his life. But since he couldn't get her, he ended up taking Lisbeth who had worked for him at his clinic. She was pretty, beautiful even, so why not? She was the one who had wanted to move in together and eventually get married. She was the one who had called his mother and introduced herself as his girlfriend without him knowing it.

"You weren't going to do it, so I had to take care of it myself," she explained to him afterwards.

She was the one who wanted all this, she was even the one who had proposed to him and he had replied with a "why not?" But now that she couldn't have it all, it was somehow his fault. So, in the end, she was the one who wanted a divorce as well and that, he was more than happy to give her.

Now he was free again even though Lisbeth did call him constantly and disturb him. Sometimes she would cry and tell him she missed him, other times she would yell at him and tell him he was a prick. He didn't know which he preferred. Maybe the latter. He couldn't stand it when women cried. If they yelled at him, he knew how to react, but crying made him so uncomfortable.

Preben drove through the plantation and spotted the hotel in the distance as he cleared the trees. He had really looked forward to this small vacation at the most expensive hotel in the country. But it wasn't the prospect of spending time in luxurious surroundings that made him drive faster, no it was the prospect of seeing *her* again. The one that got away.

Preben pulled into the driveway and passed a black limousine on its way out. He parked in front of the entrance causing the gravel to fly in the air as the tires screeched and he came to a sudden stop, nearly hitting a bell-boy. The bell-boy screamed and stared at Preben through the window with his eyes wide open and torn by fear.

Preben laughed loudly. He loved to scare people like that. He opened the door and jumped out.

"Well don't just stand there," he yelled at the boy. "Grab my suitcases."

The boy whimpered and obeyed. Preben tipped him generously as a thank you for the good laugh, then walked inside the building. It was more splendid inside than out, he thought. And he wasn't just talking about the interior decorating.

Preben smiled to himself as he spotted her in the lobby. The woman he had loved since high school. She was standing with a key in her hand talking to that smug Jacob Lomholdt.

9

DECEMBER 2013

LINE MADE it to the hotel right before noon. The train was late and she had to wait for a bus to bring her to the hotel, since she couldn't afford to take a taxi. Then she had to walk through the plantation and was almost run over by some idiot speeding by in a blue BMW, one of those egotistical cars that had no back seat and no room for children.

She had always resented people who bought those kinds of cars and now she resented them even more, since she had to jump off the road in order to not get hit by it.

Line entered the hotel and stopped just to stare. She had never been inside a building quite like this. So charming and old-fashioned, yet so modern and expensive-looking that she told herself not to touch anything in case she accidently broke it. She stood at the entrance with eyes wide open and simply stared at the interior. So tastefully decorated in light colors. The Scandinavian style.

"Miss?"

A young boy in a uniform stepped up to her.

"Yes. Sorry," she said.

"Can I take your bag?"

She looked down at her suitcase. "Of course."

She approached the counter. After she gave her name, the clerk smiled and gave her a key. "Your room is to the left, the up the stairs and to the left again."

"I sure hope it is a big one," she said.

"Excuse me?"

"Nothing. To the left?" she asked again.

"To the left. The bell-boy can show you the way."

"Follow me, Miss," the boy said and walked towards the stairs on the left.

He opened the door to the room with her keycard and they entered. She felt like a princess as she went inside, but then she froze. "Is this it?"

"What do you mean, Miss?"

"Is this all there is? This room isn't much bigger than my apartment. I thought this was the most expensive hotel in the country?"

"It is, Miss."

"So what are people paying for?" She turned and looked around. "There aren't even any flowers? Or fresh fruit?"

The bell-boy shook his head. "We never ..."

Line exhaled and threw her arms in the air. "Don't you have anything better?"

"I ... I ..."

"Look at the bathroom. I had at least expected a hot-tub. My aunt has a hot-tub in her bathroom and her house isn't even that expensive, mister. And what's with the TV?"

"You'll find the remote in the drawer," the bell-boy said.

"Now you're just saying your little rehearsed lines. Look at it. What is it? Forty inches? That's hardly anything. My mother has a forty-inch flat screen TV. Anyone can have that. This is nothing. I had really expected more from this place. Can't you do a little better than this?"

"These are the rooms we have, Miss."

"Somehow, I doubt it," she said. "What do you do when royalty and movie stars stay here, huh? I bet you have much nicer rooms for them, don't you?"

"It is an old building, Miss. It was built in 1918. Rooms were small back then. The hotel has been kept exactly like it was back then. Even the floors are old."

"Old huh? That's why they creak when you walk on them," Line said disapprovingly. "You really should consider getting new ones. I can even hear people walking around in the room next door. Is this really something people pay a lot of money for?"

Line looked up at the slanted ceiling and white painted wooden planks. She could reach up and touch it. It made her feel like she was in an attic. Line was disappointed, to put it mildly. She had expected the rooms to have high ceilings and hoped they would have an ancient stucco ceiling in the shape of a flower or maybe painted like in old churches. She loved that kind of stuff. Not this. This was just an old wooden house. Nicely painted and decorated, yes, but old and creaking.

Everything in her room was painted white, even the bed and it made her feel like she was in a mental hospital or something.

"It's hand carved," the bell-boy said when he saw her look at the wooden headboard of the bed. "It's original."

"You mean to say the bed is from 1918?" she asked, appalled.

"Yes, well the headboard is, not the rest of the bed," the bell-boy said.

Line scoffed and sat on the bed. The mattress felt good.

"Some of the rooms don't even have a bathroom," he said. "You're lucky to get one that has."

"Are you kidding me? People pay to live like this?"

The bell-boy tried hard not to smile. "Yes they do, Miss. People pay a lot of money to stay at this old hotel by the ocean. The place has a lot of history. People seem to like that."

"I guess it does have a great view," Line said.

The bell-boy nodded. Line looked at him. Why was he even still here? Oh, of course. "You want a tip!"

The bell-boy nodded. Line went through her pockets and found a coin. "Here," she said and handed it to him.

He nodded, then backed towards the door. "Lunch is in half an hour," he said before he closed the door.

10

DECEMBER 2013

HE HAD NEVER BEEN SO happy to get away. Soren Hedelund stared out the window of his room at the hotel while the phone kept vibrating in his pocket. He pulled it out and turned it off completely. It had been ringing constantly all the way up there and he hadn't answered it once. He didn't want to talk to anyone while he was here. This was his getaway. This was his chance to think everything through and figure out what to do.

What if something happens to Margit? What if she gets worse? What if the kids need you?

He looked at the dark phone. They'd have to get by without him. They would be fine. It was, after all, only for two days.

Soren opened the window and took in a deep breath of the fresh salty air. It felt ice cold on his skin, but he liked it. This was just what he needed. He looked at his watch. Lunch was only five minutes away. Then he had to meet everybody. He wondered if he should just stay in his room for the rest of his time there. Did he really have to go down there and put on a show? Did he have to pretend he was fine, pretend he was glad to see them again?

Soren exhaled and closed his eyes. There was probably no way out of it. Maybe he could just go down this one time, then pretend he wasn't feeling well and stay in his room the rest of the weekend. Maybe go for a stroll on the beach.

He had thought about disappearing on his way up here and now he was thinking about it again. Just take the train somewhere, maybe go to Germany or France? He had always loved France. His French was bad, but he could probably get by if he had to. He'd learn how to manage.

They'll find you there. They'll track your credit card and have you arrested before you know it. You know they will. You'd have to go further away. Like Bulgaria or Hungary. You liked Hungary when you were there, remember?

Did he really want to live like a fugitive for the rest of his life? Did he want to be separated from his wife and children and constantly wonder if they were alright? How could he live like that, knowing his wife was sick?

There has to be another way.

Soren closed the window and put on some nicer clothes that Margit had packed for him. She wanted him to look his best, she told him. "Show them how handsome you still are."

Soren looked at himself in the mirror. Yes, he was still fairly handsome. He had a way with women. Always had. Soren growled. Why couldn't he just have restrained himself? Why did he have to have sex with that girl?

Because she was defenseless. Because he could. Because he had done it so many times without getting caught. Because he liked it.

Soren pounded a fist on the dresser in anger, then looked at himself. "You fall, you get up. That's the way it is. Pick yourself up and move on."

Soren lifted his head, then put on a shirt and jacket. He was hungry and was going to enjoy this meal no matter what. He combed his hair and put wax in it. Then he opened a button on his shirt so his chest-hair showed a little bit.

Satisfied with his appearance, he walked out the door and down through the lobby. His heart was racing in his chest as he opened the door to the restaurant and a small crowd of people all looked at him.

"Soren?" a woman he didn't recognize at first said. "Soren Hedelund?"

He took in a deep breath and found his most charming smile. "I guess so."

"I'm Line," she said. "Line Elgaard."

"I remember you now. Still going by your maiden name, huh? Never married?" he asked and she heard a slight gloating tone in his voice.

The woman froze for a second before she answered. "No, no. But I am expecting, though." She touched her stomach gently. Soren couldn't even see a bump. She grabbed his hand and let him feel it. He couldn't feel a thing. He smiled and pulled the hand back. "Well isn't that nice. Congratulations."

Line's face lit up like a Christmas tree. Soren felt like punching her. He felt like yelling at all the staring and smiling faces in the room, telling them they were all just phony, fake and a disgrace. Telling them that they had just come here to show off and brag about all the things they had achieved, but when it all came down to it, they weren't any better than he was.

But of course he didn't. Like the rest of them, he simply smiled from ear to ear while taking the round and shaking their hands one after another, telling them; *yes, I have been very well, thank you. A paramedic. Yes it is a very giving job. Two children and a beautiful wife, yes, I have been very fortunate.*

11

DECEMBER 2013

HE WAS, by far, the most successful in the restaurant, Jacob Lomholdt thought to himself as he took a bite of the black hake they had been served accompanied by roasted cauliflower, clams and a lobster reduction. He didn't have much appetite, though and didn't quite understand why that was. The food was great, the wine was exquisite. There was nothing to comment on that account. The views were spectacular even for a man like Jacob who lived by the ocean. Everything was perfect. Yet he felt slightly nauseated and had a hard time eating.

Jacob sipped his wine and looked at the people around the table with a grin. He could tell that they felt inferior to him. Just the way they admired his expensive clothes was a true joy to him. It made the long trip up there all worth the trouble.

"So what have you been up to since high school?" he asked Preben Krogh who was sitting next to him.

"I'm a dentist," Preben answered. "I have my own clinic in downtown Aarhus where I live."

"No wife and kiddos, huh?" Jacob asked.

Preben smiled. "No. Divorced. No children."

Jacob lifted his glass of wine to salute him. "Smart man."

They toasted and drank. Soren Hedelund who was sitting across from them, toasted as well. He seemed to be drinking heavily and was already on glass number three. He hadn't said a word yet to the group.

Jacob remembered Soren very well. He had been skinny back then. The skinniest in the class. Insignificant, really. Used to want to hang out with the popular kids in class. Would do anything for them to accept him. Did whatever Jacob told him to. Even if it meant taking the blame for spying on Emma Frost when she was showering after PE. Or the times when they had beaten Niels with sticks till he was hospitalized for a week. Even then, Soren had taken the blame for all of them. Despite his efforts, he never really became a part of the group, though. Jacob never saw him as more than an outsider trying to play along. He didn't have what it took. He simply wasn't one of them. Not to Jacob at least.

"Didn't you used to wear glasses?" Jacob asked Preben.

Preben nodded. "Had laser surgery a couple of years ago. Never have to wear those bastards again. What a freedom."

He accompanied the last word with laughter. Jacob laughed too. A forced one. It really wasn't that funny. Jacob watched Preben ... scrutinized him as he ate. He had gotten chubby over the years. Too much red wine and steaks at the golf club, probably. Too little golfing. Jacob chuckled and drank some more to try to keep up with Soren on the other side of the table. Preben sitting next to him lifted his glass and toasted with Emma Frost who was sitting next to Soren. She returned the toast and toasted with Soren as well. Preben couldn't take his eyes of her, Jacob had noticed. He couldn't believe Preben still had a thing for her after all these years. It was quite pathetic.

"So what about you?" Preben asked.

"What about me?" Jacob asked as he leaned back and stretched his neck so he could look down at Preben. It was a trick he often used with his employees. Made them feel inferior and insecure. Made him feel powerful.

"Are you married and all?"

"All meaning do I have children? Then no to both. Haven't been stupid enough to fall into that trap, if you know what I mean."

Preben nodded. "I think I might. When my divorce came through I felt more relieved than ever."

Jacob nodded and lifted his glass again. "Then you and I understand each other."

"I believe we do."

Jacob drank again and shot a glance around the table. Emma Frost smiled at him and he smiled back. He had to admit, she looked great. She had gained weight since back then, but it looked great on her. She had always looked good. He had followed her career from the sidelines over the years. Her days as a reporter hadn't been very successful, but since she started writing books, her career had certainly taken off. *Smart girl,* he thought to himself and bit his lip.

If only things had been different back then. If only you hadn't ... No stop it. Don't go there. It's all in the past. Leave it there.

Jacob cleared his throat, then rose from his seat holding his wine glass in his hand. "I think we should start this weekend off properly by toasting to the class of '98. Will you all toast along with me?"

Everyone around the table lifted their glasses in the air. "To the class of '98," they said, then drank.

12

JULY 2005

THEY BOUGHT A NEW CAR. Cash. Erik had simply swiped his debit card and bought it brand new. Now they were looking at it from the window of their small apartment. The beautiful Audi A4, silver, looked so shiny among the Toyotas and Hondas in the parking lot.

"Do you think it will be safe here tonight?" Maria asked.

"I hope so," Erik said and put his arm around her. "Tomorrow we'll start looking for a new place to live. Something bigger in a better neighborhood."

He kissed her on the head and held her tightly. The police had been there earlier in the day and told him that they believed the fire was arson. That someone had set it on fire deliberately.

"It isn't uncommon in this area," they had said. "Probably just some young boys having fun. We see it from time to time. We'll have a chat with them."

Erik had been a little shocked, not because he cared about the car anymore, since he could easily afford a new one, but more because he suddenly realized they lived in a neighborhood that could be dangerous for his children. It was time to move.

"I'd like that very much," Maria said and kissed him back. "I don't feel safe here anymore."

Erik nodded. "I know what you mean."

The next day they visited a realtor and were shown a couple of houses outside of Copenhagen and they immediately fell in love with an old villa by the ocean in Klampenborg. It was half an hour drive from the city, but it was gorgeous and close to Dyrehaven, a beautiful Danish national park. It was one of the most expensive addresses in Denmark and, at first, Maria said she wasn't sure they needed all this space or to live in this fancy place with all the rich people, *the rich-people's ghetto*, she kept calling it. But once the paperwork went through and they started moving in, she took a liking to the house and the area and so did Erik and the girls. The new house had a huge yard with swings and an old tree where Erik made a tree house for them. For weeks they were extremely happy in their new home and, to their surprise, they even felt at home among all the wealthy people. Settling into the house meant they had to put off the plans of traveling around the world for a little while. They weren't forgotten, just put on hold.

They got acquainted with their neighbors and the girls soon found friends to play with on the street. The house was close to the beach and Erik and Maria enjoyed strolling on the beach and breathing in the fresh air.

It wasn't until a month later that there was a fly in the ointment.

It happened on a Sunday. The kids were playing in the yard and Erik and Maria were enjoying their breakfast on the terrace outside when there was a knock at the door. Outside stood a green bicycle courier, which was very common in that area, especially in the city of Copenhagen where they could often get to their destination faster than by car because of the traffic.

"Delivery, sir," he said and had Erik sign the papers.

Erik took the package and closed the door as the courier disappeared.

"Who was that?" Maria asked from the kitchen where she was putting the dishes in the washer after breakfast.

"A courier with a package," Erik said and went out to her. He looked for a sender but there was none.

"Who would send you a package on a Sunday? You better open it. It might be important."

Erik shrugged, then opened the package at the top. He looked into the box, then felt everything inside of him suddenly freeze.

"What's the matter, darling?" Maria asked.

Erik closed the lid of the box in a hurry so she wouldn't see it. "Nothing," he said, as he exhaled to calm himself down. "It's nothing really. Just a stupid joke. Probably just my former employees saying a proper goodbye, if you know what I mean."

Before she could protest, Erik stormed up the stairs and into his study where he locked the door behind him. Panting, he went to his desk, then poured the box's contents out on the desk. Then he gasped.

It was Buddy. His daughter's beloved teddy bear had been ripped to pieces. Even the face was scarred. Who would do such a horrible thing?

Erik reached into the box and pulled out a letter with the words:

IF YOU VALUE YOUR LIFE, KEEP QUIET ABOUT WHAT YOU KNOW.

13

DECEMBER 2013

I WAS DISAPPOINTED to see how few had been able to make it to the reunion. Only five people of the entire class of twenty-six students? That wasn't much. What was worse was that most of those who had chosen to show up were the ones I really didn't care to see again. Like that Jacob Lomholdt-guy and Preben Krogh. They both seemed to have grown into even worse versions of themselves. I had liked both Soren Hedelund and Line Elgaard back in high school. Soren I never knew very well. He was mostly the quiet boy in class. Always seemed to get himself in trouble, but that was just because he constantly took the blame for the others. He was constantly nervous and goofy when he opened his mouth. I remembered how we used to laugh at him. But now he had actually grown into a quite handsome man, even if he seemed highly uncomfortable at the table. He was drinking heavily and I wondered if he was just nervous or if he had a real problem with alcohol. Line had actually been a close friend of mine back then, but somehow after we graduated, we lost contact and I hadn't seen her since. I was glad to see her, but she seemed to be ignoring me. Maybe she was just shy? Maybe she was intimidated by my success or something. I couldn't quite figure her out. She kept saying no to wine and telling everybody with a shrill voice that she couldn't, *not in my condition.*

Then she rubbed her stomach gently. I couldn't help but chuckle at her theatrical way of telling everyone she was pregnant. I tried to keep it inside, but she noticed and gave me a look. I drank from my glass to try and drown out her disapproval.

"So who put this thing together?" I asked and looked around. "Who do we have to thank for this amazing weekend with delicious wine and food?"

Everybody around the table became quiet. People looked at each other, first to the person sitting next to them, then the person to the other side. No one spoke. Jacob Lomholdt shrugged. Preben Krogh looked at me like he expected me to be the one.

"Do you mean to say that none of us sitting here sent out the invitations?" I asked, puzzled.

People shook their heads, some shrugged. They all looked confused.

"So none of us here knows where our host is?" I asked.

They all shook their heads.

"Or even who it is?" I continued.

All eyes were on me.

Jacob Lomholdt burst into laughter. We all looked at him. He leaned back in his chair and stretched his neck, trying to look down at all of us. He was a short guy so it kind of looked like he was trying to make himself taller or something. It made me chuckle again.

"It kind of feels like were in a bad mystery-novel, now doesn't it?" He said. "Five people invited to a hotel in the middle of nowhere not knowing who their host is. I think I've heard that somewhere before. Emma, you're the writer you must know what I'm talking about."

I shrugged. "Lots of mystery-novels start like that," I said. "Like those of Agatha Christie."

"*Ten Little Indians,*" Preben Krogh said. "It reminds me of *Ten Little Indians.* Where a flock of people were invited to an island or something and then they were killed one by one."

"I believe the title of the book is *And Then There Were None,*" I said. "And the island was Soldier Island. The book was written in 1939."

"We have a *connaisseur* among us," Jacob Lomholdt said and nodded in my direction.

"Connaisseuse," I said.

"Hm? What was that?" he asked.

"I'm a woman," I said. "Therefor I'm a connaisseuse not a connaisseur."

Jacob looked at me with outrage.

"So what are you saying, Jacob?" Line asked. "That we are in a set-up of some sort, like an old mystery-novel?"

"Yeah, so what are we supposed to do?" Preben said with a slight chuckle. "Wait for whoever invited us here to kill us one after another?"

A silence broke out along the table. Everybody looked at each other pensively. Jacob Lomholdt was the first to burst into a loud laughter. Then the rest of us followed.

14

DECEMBER 2013

PREBEN WAS LAUGHING HARD. So hard that tears rolled down his cheeks. He lifted his glass and looked at his old classmates.

"Let's toast to our host, whoever it might be."

The others around the table followed.

"To our host," Jacob Lomholdt said with a deep voice.

"To our host," Line said.

Preben looked at Emma, then toasted with her as well, before he finally drank from his wine. Soren hadn't said a word and wasn't going to now. He was getting drunk and now emptied his entire glass.

"Leave room for the dinner tonight," Preben said to him.

Soren looked at him, his eyes glassy and red. Then he forced a smile before he looked down at his food and continued eating like he didn't care about what Preben had just said. In the few seconds Soren had shown his teeth while smiling, Preben had spotted a brown tooth among his front teeth. It annoyed him immensely. The man obviously hadn't been to the dentist in a long time. It was too bad since Soren had become a handsome man, but that one tooth completely disfigured his smile. It was obviously a dead tooth, one where the nerve inside had died. Either it had happened by trauma to the tooth or bacterial decay. It wasn't very obvious yet, since it was only slightly darker than the rest of them, but he needed to have it treated as soon as possible. Either he needed to have it extracted or have a root canal.

Preben shook off the thought and looked at his food. He ate some and tried to think about something else. This wasn't his problem. Soren wasn't his patient and Preben wasn't at work now.

Preben shot a glance at Emma and their eyes met for just a second. She didn't smile, so he couldn't see her teeth, but he was certain they would be perfect like everything else about her. She seemed pensive, like she was thinking about some very serious stuff.

"So Emma," Jacob Lomholdt said.

She turned her head and looked at him.

"Maybe this will be your next book, huh?" He continued. "Maybe we'll all be in it?"

Emma smiled indulgently. "I'm sure I could write many books about you, Jacob," she said. "You'd make a great crook."

Jacob paused and looked at her. Then he burst into a loud, very awkward and forced laugh. Emma didn't laugh. She stared at him like she meant it. Preben felt a pinch inside his heart. Did she know? After all these years, they had always thought she was oblivious to what had happened back then. But maybe she wasn't? Maybe she knew everything?

Could it be? No ... She couldn't have ... Was she the one who had invited them here? Why? To get rid of all of them? To let them know she knew their secret? No, it was ridiculous. How could she know after all these years? Had someone told her? No, no one would dare do that. Would they?

Preben looked around at the people sitting at the table while he was eating the rest of his food. They all knew, didn't they? Everybody around this table knew. Except for Emma, hopefully. Something was definitely off here. Something was wrong. It couldn't be a coincidence, could it? No, it was too obvious. Whoever invited them here knew their secret.

The waiter approached the table. They all looked at him expectantly.

He cleared his throat and spoke: "Coffee is served in The Green Room next door."

15

DECEMBER 2013

THE FOOD WAS ALRIGHT, Line thought to herself as she followed the others into The Green Room. Good but not great. At least not as great as she had expected it to be. It was, after all, one of the most expensive places to eat, wasn't it? It was okay to expect more from them than the usual steak houses she went to with her dates. But to be honest, she had been a little disappointed. To her, the portions were way too small. They had just been served four courses and all of them had been nothing but a small piece of fish or meat in some sauce and a little piece of bread or two tiny potatoes. How was she ever expected to get full from just that? She who was now eating for two? Line had never been to any fancy or gourmet restaurants, but she had to say, she wasn't very impressed. Every bite she ate tasted delightful, but it was like they thought she was on a diet or something, or maybe were afraid of running out of food? She didn't understand it. She left the table after two hours of eating and she was still hungry. So, as she sat down on the old-fashioned couches that looked like they belonged in a castle somewhere, she grabbed a handful of the home baked Danish butter-cookies that were placed on the center of the table, put them on her plate, and started eating greedily.

Preben Krogh looked at her like she had gone mad.

She smiled, a little shy. "Sorry. Eating for two, you know?"

"Those are really bad for your teeth," he said. Preben seemed to be staring only at her mouth. It made her slightly uncomfortable.

"They're filled with sugar," he continued like was he telling her some secret that she couldn't share with the others. "Do remember to brush as soon as you can afterwards to prevent cavities and decay."

Line nodded and continued to eat while trying to look at anyone or anything but Preben. The room was nice and light. It was packed with plants that made it look very green, indeed.

"Coffee?" Preben asked.

Line nodded as she swallowed yet another cookie. Preben poured some in her cup. They were small as well. She couldn't even get her finger in the hole. What was this hotel? Made for Pygmies? Dwarfs?

Preben kept staring at her.

"Can I help you with anything?" she asked.

He leaned over and whispered in her ear. "I know you have told."

"Excuse me?" Line said. The cookie made a lot of noise in her head when she chewed. "What are you talking about?"

"I know you've told."

Line stopped chewing. She looked at Preben, her heart racing. Then she shook her head.

"That's why we're here, isn't it?" she asked with her mouth still full. The thought had crossed her mind several times during the lunch.

"I believe so," Preben said. "I mean, look at who is here."

Line nodded and swallowed. She slurped her coffee. Line looked at Preben, then touched her front teeth with her tongue.

"If you drank your coffee through a straw, you could minimize the contact with your teeth surfaces. It can significantly limit your exposure and help keep your teeth whiter for longer," Preben said.

He was staring at her mouth again and she closed it. Suddenly showing her teeth to him made her uncomfortable.

"I never told a soul," she whispered.

Preben looked into her eyes. He scrutinized her for a while, then nodded while biting his lip.

"Well, someone clearly has spilled the beans," he said and sipped his own coffee. "And I intend to find out who it is."

16

DECEMBER 2013

HE WAS DRUNK, but somehow it didn't make him feel better. It did numb him slightly for a little while, but it was like it wasn't quite enough. He couldn't seem to forget. Now they were served coffee with an *avec*, an old very tasteful brandy that he hurried up and flushed down. He asked the waiter for one more and soon his glass was full again. Soren felt how the brandy was burning in his stomach and the room was spinning. He leaned back and let the alcohol do its job inside of him, making him forget where he was and what was going on in his life. His phone was still turned off, but every now and then he took it out of his pocket and looked at it, wondering what would happen if he turned it on, speculating if Margit and the children were alright. But he didn't dare turn it on again. He wondered if he ever would.

Soren put the phone back in his pocket and looked at his old class mates sitting on the soft couches debating something that Soren couldn't care less about. Like the discussion around the lunch table. It was so ridiculous. Who cared who had invited them to this hotel? Soren was certain it was someone at the table who simply didn't want to tell. Maybe it was just to make them all wonder, to play games with them for a little while and then reveal everything. But again, what did it matter? Soren didn't care even a little bit.

Now they were talking about old times in high school, and Soren tried to be social, thinking it might do him some good to think about something else.

"Do any of you remember Hans Frandsen?" Emma suddenly asked.

Line shrieked. "Three-legged Hans, our biology teacher?" Then she laughed. "He couldn't control that thing in his pants whenever one of the girls wore a summer dress or anything short. He was such a pig."

"So gross," Emma said.

"Did you know that he died?" Soren suddenly said.

Everyone turned to look at him like they were surprised that he was still sober enough to talk.

"He did?" Emma said.

"Yes, shortly after we graduated, Soren continued." Apparently he was killed in a car accident or something."

The conversation ceased. Soren lifted his glass of brandy and drank some. His eyes met Jacob Lomholdt's as he put the glass down. Jacob looked like he could kill him. Soren didn't care. He was a dead man anyway. His life as he knew it was over, done, finished. Might as well come clean, right? Maybe on everything?

Soren chuckled and drank again. That would show them, now wouldn't it? Go out with a bang. Take all of them with him? Maybe even get Jacob to kill him? Then he wouldn't have to do it himself.

"Kind of makes you think," Soren said.

Jacob stretched his neck. He seemed uncomfortable. Soren realized it pleased him. Making Jacob feel uncomfortable, felt good.

"Makes you think of what, exactly?" Emma asked.

Soren smiled. Preben stared at his teeth like he couldn't take his eyes off of them again and Soren noticed he clenched his fists. Soren closed his mouth. Maybe it was about time he had a little fun with his old bullies. Scared them a little like they used to scare him.

"It is kind of odd, don't you think?" Soren asked. "That he should die right after we graduated?"

Emma chuckled. No one else said anything. They all stared at Soren.

"Well it's not that odd if it was just a car accident," Emma said and drank her coffee.

"Well, as far as I know, the police investigated it as a hit-and -run," Soren said, grinning.

Jacob and Preben were both uneasy in their chairs. If it had been just the three of them, they would have jumped him.

"A hit-and-run?" Emma said. "How do you know?"

"Because I was questioned," Soren answered.

"Why would they question you?" Emma asked. She looked confused. Oh how badly Soren wanted to just tell her everything. Just to see the faces of the others. Every little part of his body wanted to just tell her right here and now.

But he couldn't. At least not like this. Instead he chose a lie:

"Because I had a car similar to the one witnesses had seen hit him. But as soon as they heard that I was in Spain at the time of the kill, they let me go."

Emma nodded but looked pensive. The rest of the party gave Soren looks to make him shut up.

"The kill? You mean they believed he was killed? Like deliberately?" Emma asked.

Soren shrugged and drank more of his brandy. "Who knows?"

"Yes, who knows?" Jacob interrupted them. "It's all a very long time ago, now isn't it? Now what about Gitte Hougsgaard our math teacher, now she was a character alright, does anyone remember her?"

17

DECEMBER 2013

JACOB LOMHOLDT FELT his hands getting sweaty. There wasn't much in this world that could make him nervous or off-balance, but right now he was feeling a little anxious. Soren Hedelund had gotten so drunk he was ready to tell almost anything, but that wasn't the worst part. The worst part was that Jacob had started fearing that this was more than just a social reunion, that whoever had invited them to this thing had done so with a purpose other than them just talking about old times.

Jacob looked at the others wondering who among them would have the audacity to try such a thing. Who would dare to do this and not fear his wrath? In the beginning, he thought it was Preben, but now he was leaning more towards Soren. He never did trust him and now less than ever. He had been so quiet during the lunch and then he suddenly started talking about Hans? Knowing perfectly well that if he ever told anything Jacob would make sure it was the last thing he ever did. They had told him then and there was no way he didn't know it still. He had been so frightened back then it had almost been too easy. But now this? What had happened to him since then that he suddenly dared to speak up? Soren had always been the quiet one, the self-effacing type. The one who wanted their approval so badly he would do anything for them.

Including killing Hans Frandsen.

He was the one who had the most to lose here, so why was he so cocky all of a sudden? He knew Jacob could destroy his life, if he wanted to. He knew Jacob would kill him if he said anything.

Luckily, Jacob had been able to turn the conversation away from their old dead biology teacher and on to their math teacher who had that shrill voice that everybody hated. While Line told them all about the time she had been caught cheating on a test, Jacob watched Soren closely. He wondered what his plan was. What his intentions were in inviting all of them up here for the weekend. And furthermore, he wondered how Soren could even afford it. He was a simple paramedic as far as Jacob knew. He didn't make much, and especially not enough to be able to afford this. And he had young children and a sick wife who couldn't work. No, money wasn't something he had. But could he have inherited some money? Jacob wondered. Yes that had to be it.

Jacob picked up his brandy and looked at Soren who smiled at him and lifted his glass to salute him. Jacob nodded politely and saluted him back before he drank without taking his eyes off of Soren.

"When she saw that I had all the answers written on my arm, she pulled me out of the classroom and yelled at me in the hallway," Line said. "It was so hard not to laugh since her voice became so shrill it sounded almost like a whistle. I swear I heard dogs howl in the distance."

Everyone laughed and Jacob joined in. "She was quite the character," he stated.

They all nodded and smiled at the memory.

"Does anyone else remember how Preben used to have this huge crush on Emma?" Soren suddenly asked.

Preben almost dropped his coffee cup.

"What?" Emma asked and looked at him while wrinkling her nose. "I never knew that."

"Well he did," Soren said with a huge grin. He emptied his brandy before he continued. "He even stole your red scarf once."

"Was that you?" Emma asked. "I loved that scarf." She smiled and put her hand on Preben's shoulder. "Well, you're forgiven." Then she laughed.

Jacob looked at Preben whose cheeks were turning red. Not because he was shy or even embarrassed, no Jacob had known him long enough to know that this was something else and something far more dangerous. It was anger.

18

JULY 2005

ERIK DIDN'T SAY anything to his wife. He stormed out of the apartment with the box under his arm, took the Audi, and drove off without a word. Kelly Clarkson sang *Since You've Been Gone* on the radio as he drove through town, but he hardly noticed. His anger made him forget everything around him.

"This is ... this is NOT acceptable," he mumbled and slammed his fist into the steering wheel of the car.

Erik was not and had never been one to lose his temper. He was a quiet and calm man who hardly even raised his voice. Being angry was unnatural to him, but for the first time in his life he had a hard time keeping his voice down. He was known as someone who would always turn the other cheek, who wouldn't even hold a grudge, but when it came to his family, he wouldn't tolerate anything.

And especially not this.

Erik parked the car in front of the apartment building in Norrebro where his partner and old friend since elementary school lived. He stormed up the stairs and rang the doorbell. He closed his eyes trying to count backwards from ten to calm himself down, then opened them as the door was opened and Jacob's eyes stared back at him.

Erik lifted the box with the ripped up teddy bear inside of it.

"Really?" he asked as he pushed his way into the apartment, knowing this wasn't something they should discuss in the hallway where all the curious neighbors would hear them.

"I give you millions, I make you a freaking millionaire and this is how you repay me?" he continued, feeling his face turn red in anger.

Jacob stared at him, then shook his head. "I need to know you'll keep your word," he said.

"So you burned my car? You took my daughter's favorite toy and destroyed it? You threaten us? Is that how we do things now, huh? What if Bella had opened the box? It would have traumatized her severely. Are you freaking kidding me? I thought we were friends, Jacob. I thought we stuck together?"

"That's what I thought too, but then you got all mushy on me and started talking about *being able to live with yourself* and all that shit. How do you think that makes me feel, huh? It scared the crap out of me, that's what it did, Erik. I'm sorry, but I need to know that I can trust you."

Erik gesticulated, resigned. "Whatever happened to just talking? Couldn't you just have asked me?"

"We're way past that now, Erik. I tried. I asked you again and again. But all I got were vague answers. That's not good enough for me, Erik. That right there is a language you and I understand," he said, pointing at the box.

"So now you're saying you'll kill me if I ever tell anything? Is that how it goes?" Erik said. "Do you have any idea how insane that sounds?"

"I'll do what I have to. I won't have you ruin everything. Not now when we've come this far, Erik. I'm not letting you do this. And I know you too well. I know you're about to break. I know you won't be able to keep it to yourself unless I make you do it. That's just how it is. You're soft Erik. You're weaker than me. Once you start thinking about telling, you won't let it go, you won't stop. So I decided to help you out a little. I did it for your own sake too. You don't want to ruin your future now. It's not just your life, it's your wife's and your kids'. I know you goddammit. I know what you're thinking even before you do."

Erik drew in a breath wanting to say something, but hesitated. Jacob was right. He hadn't been able to stop thinking about it. And there was a reason for that. It was just so wrong what they had done. So terribly wrong. It hurt him to even think about it.

"So what are you saying here, Jacob? That you'll kill me or someone in my family if I ever tell? Is that it?"

"Yes."

Erik lifted his finger in the air. "This is ... This is so ... not ACCEPT-ABLE!" he yelled.

"It is what it is. I'll protect our secret with what it takes even if it means losing your friendship."

Erik snorted. "I will not have you threaten my family, do you hear me?"

"Loud and clear. Just make sure the secret stays with you and I won't."

"You always have been an asshole."

"That might be," Jacob said. "Whatever makes it easier for you. Just remember what I said. You spill as much as a single word and you'll see what I'm capable of."

Erik threw the box on the floor and the remains of Buddy scattered all over the wooden planks. As he was about to walk out the door, he turned his head and looked at Jacob, making sure he was looking straight into his eyes.

"You have no idea what *I'm* capable of," he said, just before he slammed the door.

19

DECEMBER 2013

SO PREBEN USED to have a crush on me, I thought to myself and tried hard not to laugh while the rest of the flock shared what they knew about the other classmates who weren't present, what they ended up doing, who they married and so on. I hadn't kept in contact with any of them since back then, so I didn't have any stories to share. All I knew was what I had seen on Facebook going through my old classmates' profiles and looking at their pictures, but everybody had probably done that.

"I heard Louise became a police officer and married some police guy," Line said. "They have two children."

"I heard he left her," Preben said. "Apparently she fell in love with her therapist and came out of the closet as lesbian."

The flock giggled. "I always thought there was something about her," Line said laughing.

"Probably turned gay after I screwed her," Jacob said with a grin and leaned back in the chair. "I ruined her. It was so good no man would ever be able to top it."

"I think you're right," Line said. "After being with you she figured there was no way she could ever be with a man again."

That comment made me laugh.

Jacob smiled ironically, then drank his brandy. Line grinned. I sensed Preben's eyes were on me constantly, even if he tried to hide it and look away every time I turned my head in his direction. I kept thinking about our time in high school. Now that I knew the truth, it suddenly all made sense. But back then I had no idea he had a thing for me. I had always seen him as this pompous bastard who hung out with Jacob Lomholdt and his gang. I don't think I even thought he was capable of having feelings for anyone, let alone me. It was quite funny. I couldn't help wondering if he still felt something?

Nah, that was silly. Why would he after all these years? He had married some girl from his clinic, he had told us during lunch. It was probably just a high school thing.

"Whatever happened to your friend Erik?" I asked Jacob. "You two used to be so close."

Jacob Lomholdt paused. He cleared his throat before he answered. "To be frank, I have no idea. I haven't seen him in years."

"Didn't you start up that company together?" I asked. "The one that was sold for millions? I remember seeing his picture in the paper back then."

"Yes. We did. We started it up and sold it and then we never saw each other again."

I stared at Jacob who seemed to be sweating slightly.

"He is dead too," Soren Hedelund said.

"Excuse me?" I asked.

"Erik died in 2005. I read his obituary in the paper."

I stared at Soren wondering what the heck was going on here. "Is this true?" I asked and looked at Jacob.

He shrugged. "Beats me. Like I said I haven't seen him in years. We didn't end as the best of friends."

The atmosphere in The Green Room was getting more and more tense, I sensed. Almost strangely tense. It was like there was so much unsaid in the room, so much spoken between the lines, that I didn't understand.

"So Emma you have two children, huh?" Soren Hedelund suddenly said.

I smiled. I loved talking about my children. "Yes, Maya and Victor."

"And how old is Maya exactly?" he asked.

"Fourteen. She is turning fifteen in March, why?"

"Wow that is old. You must have gotten pregnant right after we graduated, then huh?"

I blushed. "Well, yes. Not that it is any of your business, but yes," I said, feeling suddenly a little uncomfortable. Why was he suddenly sticking his nose in my affairs? Was he trying to make us all feel uncomfortable? Or was he just so drunk he didn't care what he said to people? Did he have an agenda?

Maya's story wasn't something I wanted anyone to know about. I had been pregnant early in life and I never regretted keeping the child, even if my mother had encouraged me to terminate the pregnancy in order to not ruin my life. It had been a hard time in my life, probably the hardest I could recall. Only my dad had been supportive of me and told me to do what I felt was the right thing for me. I knew he wanted me to have the child, even if he never told me. Like me, he knew I would be able to handle it, even though I was very young myself. Even Maya's father, Michael, whom I later married hadn't wanted me to have the child at the time. He told me he wasn't ready to be a parent at the age of nineteen. But I never doubted that I wanted her and I never cared what anyone else had to say about it. To this day, I was so grateful that I had the guts to stand up to all of them. I couldn't imagine a life without Maya.

"That's very interesting," Soren said, grinning from ear to ear. "So great that you ended up having a GIRL, isn't it?" he said looking at Jacob and Preben. Something was going on between them, some sort of power struggle that I didn't want any part of.

The three others were staring at him like he had completely lost it. I found his comments a little weird and his questions a little more personal than what I wanted to share with them. Luckily, at that moment the waiter entered The Green Room and looked at all of us.

"Dinner will be served in The Red Room at half past six," he said. "Anyone who wishes to take a stroll on the beach before it gets dark outside is welcome to do so. But do it now. We're expecting a storm tonight."

I looked at him. "Say, do you know who is paying for all of this?" I asked while he took our cups and placed them on a silver tray.

"I do not, Miss Frost. All I know is that your host will be joining you for dinner later on."

20

DECEMBER 2013

"IT'S ALWAYS the most beautiful right before a storm, huh?"

Preben walked up to Emma who was standing by the window looking out at the beach. After debating for a little while who the mysterious host could be, everyone else had left the room and Preben had spotted Emma walking to the window.

"It looks so quiet out there," she said and smiled. Just as Preben had thought, she had perfect teeth. No cavities, no dead brown teeth. Probably took good care of them too.

"I was thinking about taking a walk before it gets dark," she continued.

Preben nodded and looked down at his shoes like he used to as a teenager when he got embarrassed. He felt strange, weird even. It was like all the emotions and behaviors of his teenage years, all the ones he thought he had put behind him long ago, suddenly bloomed up again inside of him. It was something he couldn't control. It made him angry that he could yet again feel like this and be out of control. He had spent so many years trying to regain control of himself and his life and never let anyone or anything hold him back.

"Sounds great," he said with a shivering voice.

You fool. You're acting like an idiot! Stop it. Walk away before you say something stupid like you always do.

"I'm sorry about all that earlier," he said. "I have no idea what came over Soren. Why he had to say all those things."

Emma chuckled. "He was drunk, I guess."

Preben chuckled too. "I guess."

Emma turned her head and looked at Preben. He felt a pinch in his stomach. Her soft eyes stared at him and he remembered how he had longed for her all those years, how badly he had wanted her back then, and how badly he still did.

"Well, I think I'll get going," she said. "Better get my jacket and probably my scarf, huh?"

Preben blushed when she mentioned the scarf. It was true he had stolen it, but not for the reason they thought. It wasn't just so he could look at it or even sniff it like some pervert. No he had used it to wrap around the girls he had sex with, pretending, imagining that they were her.

"It's cold out so you'll need it," he said, thinking again about the scarf that he always brought with him and that was waiting in his suitcase upstairs to be used again. This time for a very special occasion. This time it would be used by the very person who had always been supposed to wear it. Preben smiled while imagining himself wrapping it around her throat and tightening it till she gasped for air. He still remembered how badly it had hurt back in high school when she had turned him down. It hurt him even more now that he realized she didn't even remember. When they told her about his crush, she had said she had no idea.

How could she not know? He had asked her if he could be her date to the graduation dance. After weeks of preparing what to say. And what had her answer been? She had told him she wasn't going with anyone. She wanted to go with her girlfriends instead. How could she not remember that terrifying day, when he remembered it every day of his life since?

Now he imagined how she would fight for her life while he had his way with her. He pictured the frightened look in her eyes, the look of utter deep fear that he loved so much. That he craved like nothing else in this world. It had been a while since he had done it last. What was it? Five years? Yes, he had kept a low profile for a long time now, long enough. Ever since the police had been on to him with that girl they found in the dumpster who was a patient of his. He had gotten too careless, thought he was safe, but suddenly they had showed up at his doorstep asking all kinds of questions. They never did suspect him, but it had gotten too close. So he had needed to stop for a long time. It almost drove him nuts and made him angry and impatient with his surroundings, but it had been necessary. Now he felt that deep urge, that hunger to feel the sensation again, and doing it to Emma would be absolute perfection. It was too big of a temptation.

It was exactly what he had always fantasized about.

"Well, I'll go get my things, then," Emma said and smiled.

"Enjoy your walk," Preben said with a grin.

"Thank you."

Preben closed his eyes and smelled her as Emma walked past him and left the room. He felt a set of eyes upon him after she left and turned to look into the eyes of Jacob Lomholdt, who was standing in a dark corner of the room, lurking. He approached him with a smirk.

"You can have your fun with her later," he said. "First you and I have some unfinished business to attend to."

21

DECEMBER 2013

LINE WAS WALKING around in her room feeling anxious. Something about this whole arrangement was simply off. Line bit her nails and stared out the window at the quiet ocean. Preben had told her he thought she had been the one to tell, but she wasn't. She had kept quiet all these years even though it was eating her up inside.

That horrific, terrible dark secret.

She had kept her mouth shut and now she feared that they didn't believe her. She was perfectly aware of what was going to happen to her if they thought she told anyone. They had made that perfectly clear on that day in July 1998, two weeks after graduation.

There was only one person Line really loved in this world and that was her younger brother Arthur. But Arthur wasn't like most little boys. Mentally, he was never going to be older than a one-year old. But no matter what, Line loved him like crazy and took care of him ever since their parents had placed him in a home, not wanting to have to take care of him themselves. Line visited him very day and brought cookies for him even though she wasn't allowed to. She made sure he was happy and never lonely in that awful place.

But on that day, two weeks after graduation, he hadn't been in his room when she arrived with the cookies in her pocket. She had asked all of the personnel and looked for him outside in the park, even though she knew they never allowed the kids out there; she thought he might have gone out on his own somehow. But no. He was nowhere to be found. Anxious, she had alarmed the personnel of the home and, along with the police, they had started a search. They found him three days later tied to a tree by the lake ten miles from the home. He was thoroughly dehydrated and traumatized so badly they had to strap him down at night from then on so he wouldn't hurt himself. When they washed his clothes, they found a note in his pocket that said:

IF YOU VALUE YOUR LIFE, KEEP QUIET ABOUT WHAT YOU KNOW.

The police had asked her numerous times if she knew what the note meant and who had written it, but she had told them she didn't. That was, naturally, a lie. She knew perfectly well and she also knew that she had to obey.

Now, Line found her cell-phone and called the home.

"Can I speak to Arthur, please?"

Arthur came to the phone. "Hi sweetie. It's Line. How are you holding up?"

Since Arthur wasn't able to speak he just grunted a couple of times and then moaned. Line felt tears press behind her eyes. She was glad that he was fine but she missed him so much. He had never quite been himself again after the kidnapping and she missed that happy, sweet, childish Arthur who she used to hang out with and play with for hours. Now he was mostly angry and aggressive and she had a feeling that the personnel at the home hit him when he wasn't behaving. She had seen bruises on his back and arms, but she could never prove it, since they simply told her Arthur had fallen and bruised himself.

"That's good. Are you being a good boy?"

Arthur grunted again.

"I'll be back Monday. There is a storm coming through tonight, so don't be scared, alright? It might make a lot of noise but you'll be okay."

Arthur made a strange sound and Line thought about the baby, while caressing her stomach. Was he ever going to be able to be around it or would he be too much? Was she going to be able to visit him as much as she used to? Would she have as much time for him? Probably not.

"Now be a good boy for me, will you?" she asked.

Arthur grunted once again, then she said goodbye and hung up. She looked at her phone and went online to see the weather forecast. The storm was supposed to make landfall around six o'clock tonight beginning with the Northern parts of the country. She looked at the clock. No, there was no way she could make it out of there in time. She couldn't afford a taxi, so making it to the station would take a long time and by the time she was there, all the trains would probably be cancelled due to the storm. She would end up being trapped at the station and that probably would be more dangerous than staying at the hotel. She was scared to death of Preben and Jacob and even a little of Soren as well. Scared of what they might do to her, but she would have to get by and just make sure to never be alone with any of them.

Line looked at her own reflection in the mirror on the wall and turned sideways to better see her growing stomach, when she heard a sound coming from the hallway and gasped.

22

DECEMBER 2013

HE HAD GRABBED a bottle of champagne from the mini-bar and was drinking it from the bottle while smiling secretively to himself. This was turning out to be a lot more fun than he had expected it to be.

Soren leaned back in the soft chair in his room and drank again. It hardly tasted of anything, maybe due to the fact that he was very drunk by now, but he continued anyway. Just to keep the buzz going. Just to keep the thoughts and images away. It had started to get worse. It was like he found it hard to distinguish between imagination and reality. Just like when he had sex with that girl in the ambulance. He was certain she had told him she wanted him to do it.

He had turned on the TV in the room and they were all reporting Breaking News, telling people to stay inside tonight, when the storm would hit the country, and trying to determine which parts of the country were going to get hit the hardest. Apparently it was going to get worse right where he was, he saw when looking at the weather-map of Denmark. They had even given the storm a name. Her name was Bodil.

Soren chuckled and drank again. He really couldn't care less. He had enjoyed this afternoon immensely, a lot more than he had expected to. And tonight he was going to have even more fun. Just seeing the expressions on

Preben's and Jacob's faces when he just blurted everything out. Even Line's face was priceless. It was all worth it. So what if he pissed them off? After this weekend he would never see them again. In fact no one would see him again. Not if he went through with what he had in mind.

Soren lifted the bottle once again and drank. Lunch had been good and a lot of fun; he had a feeling that dinner was going to be even better. He couldn't wait to find out who their host really was, even if he had already guessed that it was Jacob. It had to be. He had enough money to pull something like this off. Well, so did Preben, but it just didn't seem like his thing. This kind of staging seemed more like something Jacob would orchestrate. But Soren couldn't figure out why he would do it. Why would he invite all of them here? To finish them all off like he had finished off Hans and Erik? That was certainly a possibility, but why invite Emma? She didn't seem like she knew anything at all. She seemed completely oblivious which made this whole situation so much more fun.

Soren chuckled and drank again. It was all so ridiculous, wasn't it? This entire situation, his entire life even. People were ridiculous and he realized he had stopped caring about everything and everyone.

"They can all go to hell," he mumbled to himself and drank again. A woman on the TV screen talked about how the waters surrounding Denmark was expected to rise in the coming days causing flooding and making it difficult for public transportation.

"All planes are grounded and all trains are cancelled tonight. We don't know about busses so far, but my guess is they won't be on the streets after six o'clock," she said.

Soren emptied his bottle and looked at the woman on the screen. He thought for a moment of Margit and the kids. It was going to be rough on them, but they would understand that this was his only way out, wouldn't they? Maybe it didn't matter. Once they knew everything, they would lose their respect for him anyway. They would resent and maybe even hate him. He wasn't going to stick around to see that.

Soren threw the bottle in the trash can, then walked to his suitcase and pulled out a knife, a Smith & Wesson M&P 1 Assisted Open knife, that he had bought a long time ago from some strange looking fellow in an alley in

Copenhagen and brought with him in his suitcase for his own protection. He looked at the blade and tried it on his finger to see how sharp it was. It cut off a small portion of the skin and the finger started bleeding. He sucked the blood off with a smile and put the knife in his pocket.

He had been pushed around so much in his life. It was about time he took matters into his own hands. It was about time he stood up for himself. Yes, this was indeed going to be a very memorable and fun night.

23

DECEMBER 2013

JACOB LOMHOLDT WAS GLOWING with anger. He had told Preben to take care of Soren Hedelund and make sure to shut him up once and for all while he took a shower and got himself ready for dinner. He didn't care what Preben did as long as he shut the man up. Knowing Preben, it wasn't going to be pretty and that suited Jacob perfectly. He was sick of Soren's outbursts and frankly he was sick of Soren, period. It wouldn't matter much if he was eliminated once and for all.

Jacob decided he had enough time to fill the bathtub and soak in the water for a little while, so he started filling the tub. He undressed while looking at himself in the mirror. He liked watching himself and playing with his muscles in front of the mirror. He was strong. He had been working out since the start of his teens and had joined a fitness center along with another buddy of his, Caspar who had been bodybuilding for years and who soon had Jacob hooked on it as well. They would pump themselves full of anabolic steroids and pump iron till their bodies were twice their normal sizes. Jacob still remembered how it felt when he started growing. He had always been a small kid, puny even. And when the other boys in his class started growing, he didn't really follow along. He stayed small for some reason and soon he was the smallest in his class. So growing muscles made him feel bigger and stronger than ever and he continued for years, even when his parents told him to stop. Even when he started getting aggressive and the veins became big in his throat, he didn't stop. At that point he couldn't. He loved it and had become addicted to the lifestyle. With the growing size, he experienced growing fear from his classmates and a growing power. He was feared and hated and it suited him perfectly. No one ever picked on him anymore and even his parents were afraid of him and, therefore, no longer tried to tell him what to do. Not after he punched his dad in the abdomen and he flew across the living room and hit his head on a dresser.

Today, he still did steroids every now and then, but not as much as he used to. He was still pumped and still worked out almost every day but wasn't as big as he had been back then either. He was still big enough to be able to beat the crap out of anyone he damn well pleased. And the girls seemed to like the big muscles. At least that was what they told him. When he slapped them around in the bedroom, they didn't seem so happy about it anymore, he thought and laughed.

The tub was full and Jacob got in. He closed his eyes and enjoyed the warm water against his skin. His muscles were still sore from yesterday's workout. Jacob sat still in the water with his eyes closed for quite a while and just listened to the many voices and footsteps in the old building. Next door he could hear Line's voice. She seemed to be talking on the phone with someone and Jacob knew exactly who it was. Jacob remembered with joy the day they had kidnapped Arthur from the home. It had been the easiest thing in the world. All they had to do was to give the boy an ice-cream and tell him there was more where that came from. Then he followed willingly. And the personnel at the home? Well, they were too busy drinking coffee and chatting to even notice that they left with him; hell they didn't even know Jacob and Preben were there. They had walked right in without anyone questioning them, found the poor fellow's room and talked to him. As long as the boy looked happy, then no one suspected that they weren't his friends. And frankly, no one cared. Not until he turned up in the forest, that was. Then everyone was so busy covering up for their lack of attention to the patient and explaining to the police that they did a good job at the home. What Jacob and Preben had done to the boy remained a secret since the boy couldn't talk, but it was fair to say that Jacob had his fun with him. And he managed to scare Line enough to make her silent. Jacob knew very well she wasn't the one who had talked. She wouldn't dare. And to be honest, he hadn't thought Soren would either.

Jacob took in a deep breath remembering how important it was to not let himself get too agitated about this whole situation. He didn't like the entire setup. All day he had thought about just taking off, simply leaving the hotel, but that could never be his solution. He needed to stay on top of things. There was no way he could leave them all there alone without making sure no one spilled the beans.

Jacob sighed with satisfaction when he heard the scream piercing through the walls. It was loud and delightfully filled with anxiety. It was the scream of someone dying. Jacob exhaled and closed his eyes listening to the screams. He smiled. Finally he could relax.

24

SEPTEMBER 2005

ERIK HAD it all planned out. He was going to tell. For months it had been eating him up and he needed to tell someone. So he told his wife, Maria. On a beautiful Sunday morning in September they were sitting in the yard, drinking afternoon tea in their new house overlooking the ocean. He didn't even plan to do it, he just did it. He told her everything and it felt so incredibly good to finally get it all off his chest. The twins were playing on the swing set and didn't hear their mother's gasp, nor did they notice she didn't utter a word to their dad before she finally got up from the chair and ran inside covering her mouth.

Listening to her cry in the kitchen, Erik felt more alone than ever. He didn't know what he had expected. Had he really thought she would understand? Now he realized he had made a mistake. He wanted to get it off his chest, but he hadn't thought about what it was going to do to her, to them and to their family.

He covered his face with his hands, then looked down at the girls. They were going to grow up hating their old man, weren't they? Maria was going to ask for a divorce, wasn't she? He had thought the consequences through a million times, but they never seemed as devastating as they did now that it was a reality.

After a few minutes, she came back out and sat down at the table. She sipped her tea and didn't look at him.

"I'm ... I'm terribly sorry," he said. His voice was trembling. What would she do next? Would she pick up her things, then grab the kids and simply leave without a word? Would she call the police and tell them everything?

Maria sniffled. "Well it's a little too late for that." She drank some more of her tea. Nanna screamed with joy while swinging. The waves rolled in at the beach. Several minutes went by without a word. It was excruciating. The silence was crushing.

Please just say something! Anything! Tell me you're angry, tell me you hate me for what I've done, but please just say something to me.

"So what are you going to do about this?" she finally asked.

Erik exhaled deeply. "I'm going to tell. I'm going to tell everything. I can't live with myself like this. Not with this knowledge."

Maria inhaled sharply. "Are you sure you've thought this through?" She sipped her tea without looking at him.

"I think I have ... I mean ... I don't know. I just know that it is eating me alive. I can't ... I can't sleep, I can hardly eat."

She nodded pensively. "I see."

The silence swept in between them again. Erik thought like crazy about what he had done, about what he was about to do. Was he being selfish? It was going to ruin so many lives, but still ... It needed to be told.

"Are ... will you ..." Erik cleared his throat. "Are you going to leave me?"

Finally Maria looked at him. "Leave you?" She paused. Then she shook her head. "No. This is a blow to the face, but I'll not leave you. We'll have to work our way through this like we've worked our way through so many other things." She sipped her tea again. "Yes, that's what we'll do. That's what we have to do. No matter what you decide to do with this, I'll support you in any way I can, in any way a good wife should. Just promise me that there aren't any more secrets like this one coming back to haunt us. Promise me that, Erik."

"There aren't. I promise," Erik said, feeling greatly relieved. He loved Maria so much at this moment. "Cross my heart and hope to die."

"Good."

The next day, Erik made the appointment he had wanted to for so long and as he left the house, his wife kissed him on the cheek.

"Now, go do your thing," she said with tears in her eyes. "Then we'll have to see what happens next."

"Thank you for being so understanding. You're really amazing, do you know that?"

Maria smiled. It was the first smile since he had told her the secret. It felt good to see her smile again. Maybe things were going to be alright after all? Maybe this wasn't going to be so bad? Doing the right thing was always the best; it always paid off in the long run. Erik's mom had taught him that and that was what he would stick to. Then he'd have to take the consequences afterwards. At least he now knew he had the support of his beloved wife.

Erik waved at Maria and jumped into the car. He drove off to the park where he had arranged the meeting. He parked the car on the far side of the road and got out. He locked it by pushing the remote, then put the keys in his pocket. He felt his phone vibrate and took it out. He had received a text from Maria. It simply said.

"I love you. Good luck."

Erik smiled, then walked into the road just as a car passed by and hit him, throwing him into the air. As he landed on the hard asphalt and everything went numb, he heard the tires of the car screeching and watched as it disappeared around the corner, while his mouth slowly filled with blood.

25

DECEMBER 2013

I CALLED MY CHILDREN WHILE WALKING ON THE BEACH. MAYA WASN'T IN THE MOOD FOR CHATTING SO SHE PUT VICTOR ON, BUT HE DIDN'T SAY MUCH.

"So how was Christmas shopping?" I asked. "Did you find some presents for me?"

"You already have a present. I gave you one for your birthday, remember?" He said.

"Well, as you might recall then, we also give each other presents for Christmas," I said.

"I never buy you presents for Christmas," he argued.

"I know, you didn't used to give me any for my birthday either. But that's because Maya usually buys them for you. Now we think you're old enough to buy your own. Remember we discussed this this morning as well? I gave you money and told you this was how we were going to do it this year?"

"I didn't think you meant it," Victor said.

"Well I did. I would love to get something from you this year," I said. "Just a small thing. It doesn't have to be anything big. It could be something you make if you don't want to buy me anything."

"Well I don't. But I don't want to make anything either," Victor said.

I sighed and looked out at the ocean. Victor had his own way of thinking, especially when it came to any social arrangement like Christmas. He simply didn't get the concept of repeating something every year. It was part of his condition which the doctors didn't have a proper diagnosis for but chose to call a "mild autism."

"We already did this," he would say. He didn't understand why we would do the same things year after year, just like he didn't see the need to be polite or to exchange gifts with others.

"What's the point?" he'd ask, "Why can't everyone just buy something for themselves? Then you'd spend the money on something you know you'll like instead of wasting it on something another person probably won't like." Then he'd go off to play among his trees in the yard or write strange things in his notebook like he had been doing a lot lately. I told myself to not expect too much from him, but a part of me really wanted him to get it, to understand and learn to love Christmas like other kids.

"Can't you just try? Just for my sake?" I pleaded, even though I knew it was a lost cause. Every year it was the same. I hoped this year would be different since he was now one year older, but every year I suffered a huge disappointment.

"Okay," he finally said. "I'll try."

My heart jumped with joy. "Promise?"

"Yes."

I opened my mouth to speak, when he suddenly interrupted me. "Don't say cross your heart and hope to die."

"Why?" I asked, startled.

"Stick a needle in my eye," he continued.

"A needle? What are you talking about?" I asked, puzzled.

But Victor continued like he hadn't heard me. "A secret's a secret my word is forever. I will tell no one about your cruel endeavor."

"Victor. What are you talking about?" I asked while feeling a chill. I turned and looked at the hotel in the distance. Behind it a huge mountain of pitch-black clouds had assembled. Probably the storm they had all been talking so much about. It was about time to get back. Victor's words suddenly felt sinister.

"I gotta go, buddy," I said. "Take care of granddad and Maya tonight when the storm hits, will you? And be careful."

"Okay," he said. Then he hung up. I looked at the display. I wanted to call Morten as well, but it had to wait till I was back inside. I started walking back towards the hotel when a bone-piercing scream startled me.

26

DECEMBER 2013

PREBEN WAS SCREAMING. Screaming at the top of his lungs in excruciating pain. In front of him stood a person wearing what looked like a wooden mask, like the ones he had seen in almost every souvenir-shop when he visited Kenya many years ago on one of his rare vacations with Lisbeth.

"What the HELL?" he exclaimed in anger while holding a hand to his eye where the needle had pierced through when the masked person attacked him. It had punctured the eye; there was no doubt about it.

He wondered how this person had even gotten into his room where he had been preparing himself for his attack on Soren Hedelund. He had found his gloves and was planning to simply go to his room and strangle him. But as he had picked up the gloves from his suitcase and grabbed Emma's old scarf to smell it once again and turned to go, he had looked straight into the mask. The masked person had then lifted an arm and planted a needle in his eye. The pain had made him scream and fall backwards onto the bed and suitcase. Now he was fumbling, trying to get back up and fight, but the pain held him down. Never had he experienced anything this painful in his entire life. Blood was gushing from his eye down his cheek and some ran into his mouth. The masked person wasn't moving. Preben groaned and moaned and finally got up, then stormed towards the masked person with his hands stretched out in front of him, with the intention of grabbing the person around the neck.

But as he came closer, the masked person simply moved and the result was that Preben fell to the floor with a thud. Preben whimpered in pain and got back up on his feet, but as he turned his head to look with the one eye he had left, the masked person was gone.

"Where did you go you fucking bastard?" he yelled at the top of his lungs. But the person had completely vanished. Preben turned his head frantically first one way then the other, to make sure the masked person didn't suddenly attack him from behind, but he couldn't see anyone. The door to the hallway was open and he guessed that was how the person had disappeared.

A face popped up in the doorway. It was Line. She looked terrified.

"Preben?"

"My eye!" he screamed. "My eye! It hurts!"

Line kneeled next to him and he could tell it was bad by the look on her face. A second later, Emma came running.

"What's going on here?" she asked. She shrieked when she saw the blood and held a hand to her mouth when she saw the eye.

"Oh my God, Preben. What happened?" she cried. "I'll call for an ambulance right away."

Emma grabbed her phone and started dialing. Preben whimpered as more people came to the door. Soren Hedelund staggered inside the room and looked at Preben while holding a bottle of gin in his hand.

"Oh my, that looks really bad," he said, emotionless.

Soon the clerk from downstairs came running and brought with him a bunch of other people in hotel uniforms. They all had the same expression of utter terror on their faces when they saw him. Preben heard Emma speak on the phone.

"Yes, yes of course, no, keep ice on it, okay. Good." She hung up and knelt next to Preben.

"They're on their way," she said. "They told us to leave the needle in there, it is very important. Be careful not to move it or push it around. Until they get here, we can soothe the pain slightly by putting ice on it, but without adding pressure to the needle."

"I'm on it right away," the clerk said and ran downstairs.

Preben felt dizzy from the pain. "It hurts Emma. It hurts so badly," he cried like a little child.

"I know, Preben. I know," she said and stroked his hair. "How did it happen?"

"There was someone in here," he moaned as another wave of devastating pain rolled over him.

"You mean to say it wasn't an accident? Someone did this to you?" Emma asked, startled.

"How could this be an ACCIDENT?" Preben yelled. "Are you INSANE? Do you think I came up here to sew with my own little needle that I brought with me and then OOOPS the needle FELL into my eye, huh? Is that what you thought? That's STUPID! YOU IDIOT!"

Emma drew backwards like she was afraid of him. Preben regretted his outburst; he didn't mean to scare her, he was just so ... so incredibly MAD.

27

DECEMBER 2013

LINE WAS TERRIFIED. She was staring at Preben Krogh lying on the floor with a needle stuck into his eye. Blood was gushing down his face and onto his white shirt, coloring the top of it red. Line had never been good around blood and now it made her extremely dizzy.

"Well don't just stand there and STARE," Preben yelled at them.

They all drew further backwards every time he yelled.

"Help me get up for CRYING OUT LOUD!"

Emma grabbed one arm and pulled, but couldn't get him up. She looked at Soren Hedelund who looked at Line who looked at some of the hotel personnel. Preben was a big guy and heavy too. Line shrugged.

"I can't ... I'm not allowed to lift anything heavy," she said and touched her stomach.

Soren was swaying from side to side. He lifted the bottle and drank. One of the guys in a hotel uniform took a step forward and grabbed the other arm. Line watched as they helped Preben get back to his feet, while he was groaning in pain. Line shivered every time she looked at the eye. Her stomach turned again and she felt like throwing up. There was just so much blood. Line stepped backwards while Emma and the man in uniform helped Preben get back on his feet again. He was crying in pain and whimpering and yelling at everybody.

Soren staggered towards him. He reached out the bottle of gin towards Preben. "Here. Not that you deserve it but it'll numb the pain."

Preben looked at Soren, then snorted and grabbed the bottle. He drank greedily, then wiped his mouth with the back of his hand.

"Shit. Fucking SHIT!" he yelled, then lifted the bottle again and drank from it like it was a soda.

"Keep it," Soren said. "I'll get another one."

"I intend to," Preben said hissing.

Emma cleared her throat. "So Preben, do you have any idea who might have done this to you?" she asked cautiously.

Preben drank and looked at her with furor. "Well, what do you think?" he asked.

"I don't know. That's why I'm asking you," Emma answered.

She seemed to know how to tackle Preben's behavior well, Line thought to herself. Probably learned it by raising those kids of hers.

"Did you see this person?" Emma asked.

Preben clenched his fist. "Don't you think I would have told you by now if I knew who it was? Don't you freaking THINK I would have told you?"

Emma exhaled. "There is no need to raise your voice at me. I'm just trying to help you here, Preben. That's all."

"Don't ..." Preben hissed, then drank again. "Don't freaking patronize me, Emma. I'm in pain. Can't you see I'm in pain here?"

"I do see that, but I feel like it is important that we realize that there might be someone dangerous still in this hotel right now."

"You think whoever did it is still here?" Line asked with fear in her voice.

Emma shrugged. "It's a possibility, isn't it? I mean there is a storm closing in on us. It's dangerous to be on the roads right now. Who in their right mind would go out in this weather? Plus we haven't seen a car come and go have we?"

The three men in uniform shook their heads.

"My guess is this person is still inside the hotel," Emma said.

Line gasped and looked around her. Soren Hedelund looked at her with a grin.

"Boo!" he said.

Line jumped. Soren laughed maniacally. Line grimaced.

"Idiot," she said and held a hand on her stomach while hoping the baby didn't get too agitated by all this commotion. *Can't be good for it*, she thought. She wondered again if there was any way she could get out of this place tonight. She really didn't feel like spending the night in a hotel with a madman on the loose who stuck needles in people's eyes just for fun.

Preben moaned in pain. Outside the windows the wind had picked up strongly now and the old wooden building creaked eerily. Line shivered. A tree outside the window touched the side of the house and scraped its branches across the wood. The clerk came back with icepacks.

"I brought some painkillers as well," he said.

"The ambulance is coming all the way from Hjorring," Emma said while Preben swallowed the pills and flushed them down with gin.

"Hjorring?" Preben said. "Are you kidding me? That's like an hour away!"

"Fifty minutes, they told me. It's the nearest hospital," Emma said.

Preben whimpered loudly. "Am I supposed to sit here in pain like this for FIFTY minutes?"

No one said anything. Emma nodded. "Hopefully the painkillers will help," Emma said.

"Help? Help? They don't help SHIT that's what they do. NOTHING. Look at me for Pete's sake. I'm in pain, Emma. It HURTS!"

Line looked at Preben and felt sick to her stomach again. She looked at the others present in the room.

"Where is Jacob?" She suddenly asked.

Emma looked at her. "Yes, where is Jacob Lomholdt? Has anyone seen him?"

28

DECEMBER 2013

THEY CARRIED Preben down the stairs to the lobby where they put a mattress on the floor for him to lie on while waiting for the ambulance. Soren watched them as they went out of their way to make it as pleasant as possible for the old bastard. Meanwhile the hotel personnel searched the hotel to find the perpetrator.

Soren went to his room and got a new bottle from the minibar for himself before he walked downstairs to watch the spectacle. Preben was still screaming in pain, but his screams had become more of a whimper, making him sound like a small child.

Soren couldn't help but find this entire situation slightly amusing ... seeing the big guy who was always bullying others now crying like a baby. Besides, he deserved it. Preben had deserved every little bit of this. Soren didn't pity him. As a matter of fact, he kind of enjoyed it.

Finally the bastard got to taste some of his own medicine.

Soren looked at him with a grin while the clerk brought a pillow and water for him to drink. Yes, Soren enjoyed watching him suffer and couldn't have thought of a better way to do it himself. He had wanted him to feel pain for a long time. Ever since that day in 1999 when Preben, Erik and Jacob had decided to scare Soren into remaining silent with what he knew. It wasn't like he was about to tell anyway, but for some reason they found it imperative to make sure he knew what would happen if he spoke up.

Soren had been madly in love for the first time in his life with a girl named Ida. He knew her from the bar where he worked at night. She was one of the waitresses and he had been flirting with her every day for a couple of months. Finally she had agreed to go out with him but on the night he came for her, her mother told him Ida had already left ... with some other guys who had claimed to be Soren's friends and who had told her Soren was running late and they would bring her to him.

Devastated, Soren had driven around in the small town of Ringsted where he lived back then and looked for her, but found her nowhere. Then he had gone home and found a message on his answering machine. The voice was Ida's. She was afraid; he could hear it in her voice. Soren had cried and listened to the strange message where he could hear her moan and cry, then tell them *no, no, please don't*. Then the message stopped.

"No!" Soren cried and pressed rewind to hear the message again and again. But nothing in it told him where she was or who she was with.

But he knew perfectly well who they were.

Soren drove to their houses, but found them empty. Finally, after hours of searching for them, he had gone back home to the small house he rented outside of town, thrown himself on the couch, and simply cried.

The next day he had received a phone call telling him to kill their old biology teacher Hans Frandsen.

"If you ever want to see Ida again, you'll do as you're told," the strange voice said.

Soren hadn't known what to do with himself, but knew there was no way out of this. If he went to the police, he would have to tell them everything and he really didn't want to, since he was afraid they'd find out his role in the whole thing.

So Soren had done as they told him to. He bought the ticket to Spain that was going to be his alibi, then called a friend he knew in Malaga and called in a favor. He told him to tell the police Soren was at his house on a certain day, then took his car out of the garage, drove into town where he found the biology teacher walking out of his house. It had been as easy as anything. He simply accelerated the car, hit Hans Frandsen and drove off. Then he went back home and waited for them to call.

But they never did.

Days went by and Soren didn't hear anything. He didn't eat, he didn't sleep. All he could think of was Ida and what those bastards were doing to her. He tried to call them; he tried to go to their homes and offices, only to find out that they had left the country.

"Mallorca," Erik's secretary and Preben's assistant both said. "They'll be back by the end of the month."

It wasn't until two weeks later that he realized the horror of where Ida really was. He was lying in bed late at night when he smelled it for the first time. Thinking it was nothing, maybe just that the house that needed to be cleaned better, he rolled onto his side and tried to fall asleep. But the next morning when he opened all the windows to get the smell out, he realized it didn't help at all. That was when the evil forebodings began. Something was wrong. Very wrong.

Soren walked down to the basement and that was where he found her. Sitting on a chair was Ida, gagged and strapped down. Her eyes were staring emptily into the air, her skin white with spots on it. Her wrists and ankles had deep marks in the flesh from trying to get loose. In her lap was a note.

IF YOU VALUE YOUR LIFE, KEEP QUIET ABOUT WHAT YOU KNOW.

It was at that moment, standing with the dead Ida in his arms, that Soren swore that one day he would get his revenge on Erik, Preben and Jacob.

Now he was looking at one of them who was whimpering helplessly on an old mattress making Soren sick with disgust. Soren leaned over him and whispered in his ear.

"You were coming for me, weren't you? Those plastic gloves. You had just put them on, hadn't you? So you wouldn't leave any fingerprints on my neck when you strangled me. Don't think I'm that drunk. But don't you worry. Whoever did this to you didn't finish the job. I'll make sure to do that later on."

29

DECEMBER 2013

JACOB GOT out of the bathtub and was now getting dressed in a hurry. The screams had stopped for a second and that was when he thought it was all finished, but then they had started again and continued for a little too long now.

Jacob grunted and put on his pants. He never should have left it to Preben to finish the job. It was like he always said:

If you want something done properly, then do it yourself.

Jacob was getting really upset with Preben and considered killing both him and Soren now that he had the chance. Maybe get rid of Line and Emma as well, then burn the entire place down afterwards to cover any evidence. Blame it on the storm. It was as easy as could be.

Jacob snorted and combed his wet hair back with his hand while listening to the screams coming from down the hall. He had no idea what was going on, and it pissed him off that he had to leave his warm bath to go and check it out. *Preben was going to regret this*, he thought to himself while making sure his hair looked good in the mirror.

Jacob walked towards the door angrily when suddenly there was a knock on it.

"Jacob?" a voice said. It was Emma's.

Jacob snorted. He would recognize that voice anywhere. He clenched his fists before he opened the door.

"What?"

Emma looked startled. "Sorry. Just checking in to see if you were alright."

Jacob exhaled, annoyed. "Why wouldn't I be?"

"Well the rest of us were all gathered in Preben's room and you weren't there ... so I figured that maybe ..."

"In Preben's room? What were you all doing in Preben's room?"

She looked puzzled. "Haven't you heard him screaming?"

Jacob paused. He felt confused. "You're saying that was Preben's screaming?"

Emma nodded. "Yes. Someone attacked him in his room."

"Someone? Who?"

Emma shrugged. "We don't know. He told us the person was wearing some kind of African wooden mask or something. That's all we know. He didn't see the face."

"A mask?" Jacob's voice cracked. He cleared his throat. "I don't think I quite understand what is going on here."

"Well, none of us do. But what we know is that Preben is being carried downstairs now where he will be waiting for the ambulance. He is in horrible pain. That's why he's screaming."

Jacob walked into the hallway and closed his door behind him. His anger had suddenly been replaced by a strange feeling. An eerie feeling that he didn't quite recognize, that he didn't know he was capable of feeling. Was it fear? Anxiety?

"But ... but what happened to him?" he asked as they started to walk down the hallway towards the stairs. The trees scratched their branches on the wood outside causing Jacob to shiver slightly.

"He ... well it's really ugly," Emma said. "But apparently someone stuck a ... uh ... a needle in his eye."

"A needle?" It felt like everything stopped inside of Jacob. Like his heart stopped beating and the blood froze in his veins. He drew in a couple of deep breaths and felt how his body came back to life. Jacob had a thing with eyes. He was terrified of getting something into them and didn't want people get too close to them. He never understood how people could wear contacts and poke their finger in their eyes every day like that. To him, it was the most repulsive thing in the world.

He followed Emma down the stairs while his heart started hammering in his chest. Preben's scream increased in volume and the thought of what had happened to him made the screams even more unbearable to Jacob. He was getting hot now and had trouble breathing properly.

"He's right down here," Emma said and turned the corner.

Jacob followed. Then he stopped. He stared at Preben lying on the mattress on the floor with the needle sticking out of his eye, screaming in pain.

"Jacob?" Emma said, concerned. "Are you alright? You look pale. Do you want to sit down?"

He opened his mouth to speak, but there were no words. Only a warm mass of vomit that spurted out onto the floor and all over his expensive Armani shoes.

30

SEPTEMBER 2005

HE WAS SUPPOSED to lose his life, but he didn't. That was all he could think of when the doctor spoke to him the very next day, telling him he had suffered what they called a *coup injury*. The right side of his skull cracked open when it was slammed against the asphalt so hard that it had fractured in several places.

"You have two broken ribs as well," the doctor continued while Erik stared at him indifferently. He might as well have told him he had eaten potatoes for breakfast. All Erik could think about was the fact that he had been cheated, he was supposed to die and instead he was left with this.

Erik looked at Maria who was standing next to him with a smile meant to be sympathetic, but to him came off as condescending. Erik blinked a lot to try to focus better, but the sight of his right eye was blurred by curtains of red stripes. *Blood*, he thought to himself. Erik tried to move in the bed; he pulled the covers to the side even though his arm hurt so badly that he almost gave up. Then he tried to swing his body out of the bed, but it didn't obey. He tried again, but his legs didn't move an inch. Erik panicked.

"I ... I can't ..."

The doctor stopped him. "No, Erik. You can't move your legs. You have been paralyzed from the waist down."

Erik stared at the doctor who suddenly looked like he actually had potatoes in his mouth. He blinked his eyes again.

"You have suffered brain damage as well. It might cause you to see things that aren't really there. You'll have trouble remembering things and you might have some speech problems as well, but time will show how bad it really is." The doctor looked at Erik and smiled. Erik thought it looked like he moved in slow-motion. Were those potatoes or were those his ears?

"You were lucky, Erik. Usually a coup injury causes a person to become mentally impaired, but it seems you might get away with just minor issues."

Maria nodded slowly. "Like the memory loss and speech problems?"

"And hallucinations, yes."

Erik felt like he had left the room and they were talking about someone else. He wanted to speak, but couldn't find the words. Not the right ones at least. He could come up with a lot of words, just not the ones he wanted to use.

"Potato," he finally said after searching his mind.

The doctor and Maria looked at him for a second, then looked at each other again.

"How bad will the speech problems be?" she asked.

"Well you just witnessed it. He will have a hard time finding the right words to say what he means. It'll get better though, but he probably will never be like he was before. In the beginning, saying even simple things will be a struggle for him."

Maria nodded pensively while looking at Erik. He felt like screaming, yelling at everybody in the room, at the world, at God for keeping him alive.

"You'll get help, don't worry," the doctor said and put a hand on her shoulder like she was the one who was hurting here.

Erik wanted to yell at them that he was right there, that he was the one panicking right now, he was the one trapped inside of this strange body that he felt like he no longer knew. He wanted to cry for help, for compassion, but he didn't know what to say or how to say it.

"Bitch," he said instead.

Maria and the doctor looked at him again quickly, then at each other. "The government has a special program for people in your situation."

Your situation? Her situation? What about my situation? I'm the one who can't move. I'm the one who can't even freaking speak!

"Beetroot!" he yelled.

Maria and the doctor both turned their heads. Maria smiled, then leaned over and kissed his forehead gently. "I'll get you potatoes and beetroot, dear. Don't you worry. I'll take care of you."

Erik looked at the woman he had loved for so very long and for the first time in their marriage he wanted to punch her in the face. But he didn't. Instead he turned his head away with a grunt.

God, why did you do this to me? Why didn't you just kill me when you had the chance? I'm in hell and I have no idea why.

31

DECEMBER 2013

BODIL, the merciless storm was right above our heads now. The old house was cracking and creaking and trees were falling to the ground outside, one after another. I was standing next to Line, looking out the window at the raging storm while the hotel personnel were washing the floor where Jacob had thrown up. They had searched the entire hotel, but found no one who wasn't supposed to be there.

I looked at Jacob quickly as he was sitting on the couch in the lobby. He had taken his shoes off and the clerk told him they would clean them. Now he was staring like he was paralyzed at the hurting Preben who was still lying on the mattress, moaning in deep pain. At least now I knew that Jacob wasn't the one who had done this to Preben, which had been my first impulse, but seeing his reaction made me certain he wasn't able to do this.

Cross my heart and hope to die, stick a needle in my eye. That's what Victor had said on the phone. Victor knew. Somehow, he knew this would happen.

I turned my head and looked out the window again, anticipating seeing the ambulance approaching in the distance any moment now. It was getting dark and the storm was getting stronger by the minute. Branches and leaves were flying through the air. A tree was knocked down in the hotel's driveway. Line gasped as it landed in the gravel and was pulled closer to the building by the wind. I looked at my phone to see what time it was and realized I had no reception any longer. I pushed a couple of buttons and tried to walk to the other end of the lobby to see if I could get it back, but it was gone.

I exhaled and put it back in my pocket. I went back to Line.

"Do you have any reception?"

She didn't answer, but continued staring out the window with a frightened look on her face.

"Line," I said again and pulled her shirt.

"What?"

"Do you have any reception on your phone?"

She reached into her pocket and pulled out her cell. She looked at the display, then shook her head.

"That's what I thought," I said. "We've been cut off from the world."

"Luckily the road is still open for the ambulance to get through," she said.

Her last words were accompanied by a loud crash that sounded like it was coming from outside. Line screamed and we both turned to look. A big tree had fallen right into the wing next to ours. Its branches had gone through the roof and into some of the rooms. Everybody in the lobby looked at each other with great confusion.

"I'll go see how bad it was," the clerk said with a shivering voice. "There is a door leading to the next wing upstairs."

He went upstairs and came back a few minutes later with a worried look on his face. "Two of the rooms upstairs are hit," he said. "Nobody used them so we're in the clear. But it's gonna be expensive to fix."

"Are there any other guests here at the hotel besides us?" I asked.

The clerk froze.

"There is, isn't there?" Jacob said and got up from the couch. "We're not alone!"

The clerk shook his head.

"Our host is here," I said. "Am I right?"

"Yes. You're right," the clerk said. "I wasn't supposed to say anything. It was going to be a surprise once dinner was on the table, then your host was supposed to show up."

The lights went out for a short minute, then came back on, then flickered a couple of times before they were steady again. Line shrieked.

"So where is our host now?" I asked. "It might be a good idea to have all of us gathered in one of the safer rooms down here, like the Yellow or Red room in case more trees should fall upon the building."

The clerk looked perplexed. "Yes of course. I'll go and tell your host."

"We'll keep an eye out for the ambulance," I said. "It shouldn't be long now."

"Okay," the clerk said and bit his lip. "Guess I'll go upstairs again, then. Be right back."

I exhaled and sat in one of the chairs feeling a little lost and maybe a little scared as well. This whole situation frightened me, no that was putting it too mildly, it creeped me out. I kept wondering who had done this to Preben. Could it have been our host? Could he for some reason have brought us here to hurt us? Was it really like one of those mystery books? If that was the case, wouldn't Preben be dead by now?

Another loud crash pulled me out of my stream of thoughts. Line screamed and ran to the window by the door to see better. I joined her. A huge tree trunk had fallen and was now blocking the road completely.

"*Now* we're cut off from the world outside," Line said.

"There is no chance in hell that an ambulance will be able to get through there," I said with a deep sigh. We were completely on our own.

32

DECEMBER 2013

PREBEN HEARD the crash and felt deep within him that this was something big, this one was different than the other crashes. Still in pain, he managed to lift his head enough to be able to look at Emma and Line. Just by the look on their faces he knew this was bad. This was really bad.

"What happened?" he asked, then put his hurting head back on the pillow.

No one answered.

"WHAT HAPPENED?" he asked again, this time yelling. "What was that crash?"

Line cleared her throat and looked at him. "Well it ... uh ... it was another tree that fell."

"Where did it fall?" Preben asked. "WHERE?"

"Across the road," Emma said. "I'm afraid it is blocking it. I don't think the ambulance will be able to get through ... I'm so sorry, Preben."

Preben wanted to close his eyes, to shut out this nightmare for just a second, but he couldn't. He tried so hard not to move his eyes at all since it was so incredibly painful to do so. Even blinking hurt so bad he would scream. He clenched his jaw and bit down even though he knew it was bad for his teeth and could scratch the surfaces.

"You're kidding me, right?" he asked with an almost maniacal laugh. "Please tell me you're kidding."

Emma exhaled. It wasn't a sound he wanted to hear. "Please don't exhale. Please don't sigh. Just tell me you were joking. Tell me it was some cruel and inappropriate joke on your part."

"Preben ... I ..."

"Just SAY IT, goddammit."

"It was a joke," Line answered.

Preben groaned and took in a deep breath.

Don't think it. Don't even think it. Don't think about how long it is going to take, don't imagine it's gonna take all night, don't even think it.

"Of all the times a storm could have hit, why on earth did it have to hit tonight of all nights?" Preben yelled.

"Try and stay calm," Emma said. "For your own good. I'm sure the ambulance will find another way to come here."

"How?" Soren asked. "By boat? In a storm?" Then he laughed. "No Preben old buddy, you're stuck here with us all night. Does it hurt? I bet it does." Then he laughed again and drank more from his almost empty bottle.

"Maybe you should lay off the booze for a little while," Emma said. "We're gonna need everyone to be ready for whatever might come tonight."

Soren grinned. "Oh I'm ready alright. I'm ready for whatever will come my way. Don't you worry about that."

Preben tried to shut him out by not listening to him and all his crap. More than ever he wanted to kill him, to finish him off like he wanted to do back in 1999 when they were afraid Soren was going to tell. Preben had wanted to burn down the house he lived in with Soren inside of it. But Jacob had thought of another idea.

"This is much better," he had said. "Much more cruel. And no one will ever suspect us."

They had put her in his own basement and once she turned up dead, Soren was accused of killing her. The police couldn't prove anything though, since they found none of his fingerprints or his DNA on her body or on the duct tape they had used to tie her down. So he was acquitted.

Then they used him to kill Hans Frandsen and Preben admitted that this was way better than simply killing Soren and then having to deal with Hans Frandsen afterwards. Preben thought Soren would go down for the killing of the old biology teacher, but somehow he found a way out of that one as well. It annoyed Preben back then and still did. More than ever. He never liked Soren and never wanted him to be a part of anything they did. He knew Soren was bad news from the beginning, he was way too weak to be in on what they were doing, but the others wouldn't listen. Especially Erik, he had liked Soren and wanted him in.

How could he have been so blind, so stupid?

Preben groaned again. A thought had entered his mind and he couldn't get rid of it. Ever since he stood in front of that masked person in his room, he had been wondering who was hiding behind it and now, looking at Soren standing next to him, he felt suddenly overwhelmed with a certainty that it had to be him. It had to be Soren. Only he would be such a coward and hide behind a mask instead of facing his victim like a true man. But he wasn't going to get away with it. Preben might have fallen, but he wasn't dead yet.

33

DECEMBER 2013

"THIS HAS GOT TO STOP!" Line yelled. "I want to go home, I want out of this place."

She was no longer able to hold herself together and keep calm. When the tree crashed down and blocked the road, the panic had slowly spread throughout her body. Emma was trying to calm her down, but it didn't help. All Line could think about was the baby in her stomach that she was afraid she would never get to see.

"How are we going to get out of here?" she asked, looking at Emma. "Tell me how? How Emma?"

"We'll just have to wait," Emma said with a soothing voice.

"Wait? How are we supposed to wait here when there is someone out to get us? Huh? Can you explain that to me? We're like sitting ducks waiting to get killed."

"You have to keep calm, Line," Emma said harshly. "We can't lose it. Just be happy you're not the one on the mattress with the needle in your eye, okay?"

Line looked at Preben who was sweating with pain. She bit her lip, then took in a deep breath. Emma was right. At least she wasn't the one in pain.

"There is nothing we can do," Emma said. "Except stay calm and collected. The paramedics will find a way. The storm will stop eventually and we'll all get to go home. It's all gonna be just fine."

Line nodded while staring at Preben. She could understand why someone would want to hurt him. She had dreamt about hurting him for many years. He probably had a ton of enemies. Maybe that was all this was? Someone getting back at him for something he had done a long time ago? She shot a glance at Jacob sitting on the couch looking pale. Chances were that he would be the next if there was to be one.

Jacob sighed. "Where is that clerk?"

Soren giggled. Emma shrugged. "It is odd," she said. "He has been gone for like half an hour."

Line could hear her own heartbeat. She tried to calm herself down, but that only made it worse.

If something happened to the clerk, then something could happen to any of us.

"Where is he?" she asked as she walked towards the stairs and looked up. She tried to listen, but there was no sound.

"Maybe he just went into the kitchen to check on dinner. They're still working on getting it ready in there," one of the two bellboys sitting in the lobby said.

Line inhaled. Yes there was a nice smell of food in the building. But could anyone eat under these circumstances? She touched her stomach. Well maybe just a little. She had to think of the baby too. But it was hard to keep an appetite with Preben wailing in the building.

"Maybe the bell-boy is right," Line said.

Emma looked at her quizzically. "But we saw him walk up the stairs," she said. "Wouldn't he have to come down here in order to go into the kitchen?"

They all went quiet. Line looked out the window into the deep darkness that surrounded them. The moon was shining brightly between passing clouds and she could still see branches sweeping across the hotel's driveway. The building was still creaking loudly and every now and then she wondered if it would even be able to sustain the strong winds.

Line's stomach growled. The thought of food made her hungry all of a sudden. She hoped they weren't preparing one of those long meals with small dishes again. Line really wanted a real meal with enough to eat on her plate. Plus it would be a nice break for them to forget their circumstances. She looked at Soren who had been to the hotel bar and gotten himself a couple of drinks that he shared with Preben. She felt a little jealous. She desired a drink more than anything right now. Just to make her forget.

Line sighed and closed her eyes. She imagined herself holding her baby in her arms. She had dreamt of becoming a mother for so incredibly long. Nothing was going to get in the way of that now. Nothing and no one.

One of the waiters from the restaurant came into the lobby carrying bottles of water. Emma took a couple and gave one to Line who drank greedily.

"So what do we do now?" Line whispered to Emma. "Do we just stay here in the lobby all night or should we go into the restaurant and get something to eat, or what?"

Emma shrugged. "I don't know." She glanced at Preben. "We can't leave him here in case whoever did it returns to finish the job."

"Of course not," Line said without meaning it. She really didn't care what happened to that bastard, but could hardly say so out loud. She was getting hungrier now and could smell the food from the kitchen. She found a chair to sit on, but it wasn't very comfortable. It annoyed her to know that right next door in the Green Room she could sit down comfortably.

"Why don't we just transport him next door?" she asked.

"I'm afraid it will be too painful for him to be moved," Emma said.

Line growled.

So what if it is painful? The guy inflicted pain on all of us for years without caring. He's a sick bastard who no one will ever miss if he dies. If you only knew, Emma. If you only knew you, wouldn't be so eager to help him out.

She wanted to say something, but held it back. Emma wouldn't understand. She didn't know what Line knew. Meanwhile, Line's stomach was almost hurting with hunger.

"I have to go to the bathroom," she said and stood up.

"There's one right down the hallway," Emma said and pointed.

"I'll use the one in the restaurant instead," Line said and started walking. "Be right back."

34

DECEMBER 2013

SOREN WATCHED Line leave the lobby through the door to The Yellow Room where they had enjoyed their lunch. Soren didn't feel hungry at all. He kept drinking to make sure he didn't feel anything. But it was getting harder and harder to drown out the fear and the sadness. The fact was, he still had no idea what he was going to do.

Soren looked at Preben and grinned. Then he stuck his hand inside his pocket and felt the knife.

Just do it, Soren. Finish him off. You've wanted to do this for so long. You've dreamt about it, haven't you? This is your one chance. You'll never get it back. Do it for Ida. You have nothing to lose. Nothing.

Preben was squirming on the mattress. "Give me a drink," he moaned and looked at Soren. "Give me something for the pain, please?"

I'll give you something for the pain, alright.

Soren grabbed the handle and was about to pull out the knife when suddenly he was interrupted by a scream and a thud coming from upstairs. Everybody in the lobby looked at one another. Except Preben who didn't seem to care and was still screaming for painkillers. Soren gave him his drink and he guzzled it down with a groan. Soren's eyes met Jacob's.

"What was that?" Emma asked.

She walked closer to the stairs and looked like she was listening. Her eyes were anxious. Soren felt his heart rate go up as well.

The two bell-boys looked at each other with fear.

Soren got up from his chair. "I'll go up and check," he said.

"You shouldn't go alone," Emma said, concerned.

"Of course not," Soren said with a grin. "I'll take Preben with me."

"Very funny," Preben groaned.

Soren turned his head and looked into Jacob's eyes. Jacob was shaking his head.

"Jacob can go with me," Soren said, feeling the handle of the knife between his fingers in the pocket of his pants.

Jacob looked at Soren like he was making up his mind. "Okay," he said and stood up. "I'll go with you."

Soren smiled from ear to ear while Jacob approached him. He put his hand on Jacob's shoulder.

"Hurry back," Emma said.

"Oh we will," Soren said as they walked closer to the stairs. "Probably won't take long."

Just as long as it will take to bleed to death from a stab wound.

Soren made room for Jacob on the stairs. "After you," he said.

"Let's just get this over with," Jacob said with a tired voice and walked up the first couple of steps.

Soren watched him closely as he moved. He scanned his back for the perfect spot, the one right between the shoulder blades where he was planning on stabbing him. If done right, he would die instantaneously. But Jacob was broad between the shoulders and very muscular. It was going to take all of Soren's strength to push the knife through.

Soren followed Jacob up the flight of stairs with his eyes fixated on his back imagining how he was going to do it and grinning at the thought of how wonderful it was going to feel. Finally, finally he would get his revenge. On both of them. Once he was done with Jacob he would move on to Preben. It was almost too easy.

Like it was meant to be. Like the universe or God or the devil or whoever reigned in this cruel world had planned it all for him.

35

DECEMBER 2013

THEY REACHED the end of the stairs and started walking down the hall-way, going from room to room, opening the doors to look inside, then closing them again. Jacob didn't care much about this clerk and, frankly, didn't care if they found him dead or alive. But he did care about Soren and still wanted to get rid of him. This was an excellent chance.

"Anything?" Soren asked when Jacob poked his head inside one of the rooms. They had borrowed a master key to all the rooms from one of the bell-boys downstairs and Jacob was the one holding it and opening all the doors. Soren was right behind him and it made him feel slightly uncomfort-able. He didn't like the way Soren grinned when he turned his head and looked at him and he didn't like the look in his eyes either. Jacob couldn't wait to put his strong hands around his neck and just strangle him. Shut him up once and for all.

Jacob shook his head. "No. Let's try the next one."

They walked down the hallway and stopped in front of the next room. Jacob wondered when he should strike. He was going to be careful not to do it too early. He wanted them to reach further down the hallway so no one downstairs would hear it when he made his move. Jacob was way stronger than Soren so he wasn't expecting much of a struggle, but still didn't want to take any chances.

"Did she scream?" Soren suddenly asked as Jacob put the key in a new door. Jacob froze in the middle of swiping the key-card.

"What are you talking about?" he asked. "Don't go all weird on me now. I need your help with this."

"You know very well what and who I'm talking about," Soren said, sounding suddenly very sober.

Jacob swiped the card again, the door clicked and he opened it. He turned and looked at Soren. "Don't go there, Soren. Not now, okay?"

Jacob turned with the intention of walking into the room, but Soren stopped him by pulling his shoulder. He took the keycard out of his hand. "I want to know."

Jacob exhaled. "No you don't."

"Let me be the judge of that. I want to know what you did to her."

Jacob peeked inside the room. "Hello?" he said. No answer. The room didn't look like there had been anyone living there. He closed the door again, then turned to face Soren.

"What did you do to her?" Soren asked again. His lips were shivering as he spoke. His eyes blistering with hatred. "You tied her up in my own basement where she died of dehydration. But what did you do to her. Did you ..." Soren was gritting his teeth. "Did you ... rape her?"

Jacob really didn't want to have this conversation now and pushed Soren aside and started walking towards the next rooms. They were almost at the end of the hallway now and maybe far enough for him to do it there. So what if they heard something? He would just kill all of them if he had to. That was the best solution anyway.

"I'm not talking about this with you now," Jacob said harshly.

"Then when? For all these years I've been wondering. For every moment of my life ever since that day she was found, I have wondered what went on before you tied her down. What horror did you expose her to? The police said she had intercourse prior to being tied down but found no semen inside of her. Did you rape her using a condom so you wouldn't leave DNA, huh?"

Jacob chuckled. "You really have a vivid imagination don't you?" He leaned over and pulled Soren's shirt. "If I were you I'd leave it, alright? It's all in the past. Let it stay there."

Jacob let go of Soren's shirt, then turned his back on him and started walking again. In front of him, there was a new door. It was much bigger than the others. A double door with hand carved wood.

"This must be the Honeymoon Suite, don't you think?" he said and studied the beautiful old door. This was the perfect place. He would make Soren go inside with him, then kill him when they were inside. "Give me the key-card please." He said and reached out his hand without looking at Soren.

Soren reached into his pocket, pulled out his knife, and planted in between Jacob's shoulder blades. Jacob screamed and fell forward into the door. It wasn't locked and it opened to reveal a huge room behind it. Jacob fell onto the carpet with a loud bump. The pain in his back was excruciating, yet he managed to lift himself up on his knees and turn to look at Soren behind him.

"What the HELL?" Jacob yelled.

Soren seemed surprised that Jacob was still alive. He stared anxiously at him. "I hate you!" he yelled back. "I hate you, I hate you, I hate you. All of you. All of this! You've ruined my life!"

Then he turned around and ran. Jacob gritted his teeth in pain, then yelled after him:

"That's right, buddy. You better run. Once I get my hands on you, you're done! Do you hear me? You're done!"

36

SEPTEMBER 2005

"WHAT'S THIS?"

Maria threw a newspaper on the table in front of Erik. He was sitting in his office, which had become his entire world, since he refused to go anywhere anymore, let alone let anyone see him.

Erik looked at the paper and the article Maria wanted him to see, then he pushed it away, grabbed the wheels of his chair and rolled away.

"Toothpaste," he said.

"Listen, Erik. I know this isn't easy for you. It is hard on all of us. Especially the girls since you refuse to see them. But to write your own obituary and run it in the paper, that's just sick, Erik. It's sick. I've had a ton of phone calls from all kinds of people this morning telling me how sorry they are for my loss. Not to mention all the flowers that keep coming and now fill our entire dining room downstairs. I have no idea what to do with them."

Erik didn't look at her. He stared at the curtains that hadn't been pulled aside in the office since he came home from the hospital. Maria had put his bed in there since he couldn't get up the stairs anymore, and it suited him well to be alone at night as well. He didn't want to see any of them ever again, but he depended on her help to get in and out of the chair. But not for long. He would find a way to make himself independent again, so she wouldn't have to stay with him out of pity. He wanted her to go. He wanted her to go out into the world and find herself a proper husband. One who could take care of her the way she deserved. She was still so beautiful and he was so ugly after the crash had severely disfigured his face. He wanted to tell her all this, but he couldn't find the words. Instead, he always ended up yelling at her. Mostly really bad words since they seemed to be the only ones he could say lately. That or random things like toothpaste or pencil. The worst part was that he had lost control over it. He had no idea what would come out of him next. And he could tell that his words hurt her. Even if she knew he couldn't control it, she was hurt by them. It was going to get better over the years, the doctor had told him, but he wasn't sure he was able to wait that long. He wasn't sure it was fair to Maria to have to wait for that. What if it never got better? Was she supposed to take this verbal abuse over and over again until he finally died and she got her life back? No, this was no life for her.

Erik had written a letter to her explaining all of this and now he handed it to her.

"What's this?" she asked. It was funny how she still seemed to be expecting him to be able to explain himself or suddenly, somehow regain control of his brain.

"Toilet paper," he said.

Close enough when he wanted to say letter.

Maria tore the letter open and started reading. He observed her expression. She shook her head.

"You want me to go out and find another man?"

Erik shook his head, then grumbled something no one would be able to understand, let alone himself.

"Don't be ridiculous," she said and ripped the letter into pieces.

Erik couldn't tell her, but somewhere deep inside he was relieved. But it didn't last long. A few months later he realized that Maria had only pretended to not want to be with other men. Maybe to not hurt him. Maybe she had meant it, but later changed her mind. Either that or she had finally had enough of him and his yelling ugly things at her and calling her the most atrocious things. Since Erik wasn't able to perform in bed, he couldn't blame her, but it was hard for him to lie in his bed and listen to her having other men over, enjoying a glass of wine in front of the fireplace, and having sex on their couch while the children were sleeping upstairs. He really hadn't thought it would affect him like this, but it did. It hurt him badly and he tried to tell her by writing her another letter, but she just looked at him and tilted her head.

"You're the one who told me to do it, remember?"

He wrote her another note while she was standing next to him. I DON'T LIKE IT ANYMORE. PLEASE STOP.

Maria shrugged. "So what are you going to do about it, huh? You're stuck to that chair and I'm the only one who can help you. I'm the only one who bothers with you even though you do nothing but yell at me and call me dirty names."

PLEASE LEAVE ME. I WANT A DIVORCE, he wrote.

Maria laughed, then took the piece of paper and rolled it up. "Oh no you don't," she said and stroked his head. "I'm staying here. You know as well as I do that if we get divorced, I get nothing. You made sure of that when you made me sign that prenup. I thought it didn't matter back then since you had nothing. But now you have everything and I helped you get it. I worked for this money too, sweetheart. I sacrificed everything for you. And even if I can't have the ending I was hoping for, I'm gonna take what I can get. I own part of this money as much as you do and I'm not turning my back on it. So this is how it is going to be from now on, buddy. I'm in charge and you answer to me."

Then she turned her back on him and walked out of the office, locking the door with the key behind her.

37

DECEMBER 2013

I HEARD another scream coming from up the stairs and it creeped me out. Line hadn't returned from the restroom yet and I was worried about her as well. Why was it taking her so long? Couldn't she find it?

Now that another scream sounded from upstairs I looked at Preben who still didn't seem to care, then at the bell-boys.

"What was that?" I asked.

"Who cares?" Preben yelled.

I took my phone out of my pocket once again and looked at it. Still no signal. The winds were howling outside and the gusts seemed to get stronger every minute now. To be frank, I really didn't know what to do next. Should I go up there and see what was going on? But that would mean leaving Preben and Line. Could I ask the bell-boys to go or maybe run into the kitchen and get someone else to do it?

Next thing I knew, I heard steps coming from upstairs. It sounded like someone was running. Then I heard what I thought sounded like Jacob's voice yelling something. Was he the one who had been screaming? Or was it Soren? I heard more steps running and yelling again. I looked at the bell-boys. They were both maybe around twenty years of age. Not big in size, but one of them at least seemed like he could protect me.

"You," I said and pointed at him.

"Me?"

"Yes, you. I want you to come with me upstairs and see what is going on. What's you're name?"

"Jon."

"Jon you come with me." He got up and I was glad to see that he was bigger than he had appeared sitting down. I looked at the other guy. "What's your name?"

"Jesper."

"Jesper, you keep an eye on Preben Krogh here and make sure he is alright while we go upstairs and see what the heck is going on. Okay?"

Jesper nodded. "Sure."

"Follow me, Jon," I said and walked up the stairs.

We reached the end of the stairwell. I looked at Jon.

"It's kind of scary," he said. "The hallway reminds me all of a sudden of the one in *The Shining*. Remember that one? You know with Jack Nicholson? The scene with the boy who sees two girls standing at the end of the hallway?"

I didn't answer. Of course I remembered. Who could ever forget? I had seen that movie over and over again as a teenager and I had had the very same thought the first time I looked down the hallway with the carpet and flowery old wallpaper on the walls.

"Try not to think about it," I said and started walking. "Jacob? Soren?" I called again and again, but no one answered. I tried to listen for footsteps or anyone talking or screaming, but still nothing. I knocked on some doors and called their names again.

"There doesn't seem to be anyone here," Jon said. He seemed more confident now and walked with fierce steps in front of me. He pulled a couple of handles to rooms, but they didn't open.

"Hello?" he called out. "Is there anyone up here?"

"How far down did the trees hit?" I asked.

"That was much further. In the other wing. That section wasn't in use this weekend. I don't think there'll be anyone over there."

"Can you go through this wing to get to the other or do you need to go outside?" I asked and knocked on a door. "Hello? Is there anyone in there?"

No answer.

"You can go through at the end of the hallway. There is a fire door leading to the other wing. Only the staff uses it and you need a keycard."

"So someone could run out that way?"

"If they have the key, yes."

I wondered if Soren and Jacob could have gone through that door. They had a Master key that worked on all the rooms. I didn't know if it worked on that door as well.

I knocked on another door, then continued to walk as I spotted a door with a handle and pulled it.

"That's just the cleaning closet," Jon said just as I opened it and a body fell on top of me.

Then I screamed.

38

DECEMBER 2013

LINE WAS STUFFING her face with foie gras. She was eating with her fingers. Bread and foie gras. Meanwhile the chef and the two others working in the kitchen were watching her while working.

"Oh this is so good," she moaned. "This is sooo good."

"I'm glad you like it," the chef said with a grin while sautéing mushrooms in a pan. It smelled heavenly.

"Could I get some of those as well?" she asked.

"Sure." A second later, a plate landed in front of her. She found a fork and started eating them. It was like they melted on her tongue.

"So what's going on out there?" the chef asked. "Someone told me a guy was hurt? Something with his eye?"

Line closed her eyes and tried not to think about them. She had long forgotten all about the others in the lobby. She really didn't want to go back. She opened her eyes and swallowed the mushrooms. "Yeah, one of the guests had a needle stuck in his eye."

"Ouch," the chef said.

"It's pretty bad. We're still waiting for the ambulance, but I don't think it can come through since a tree fell across the road and it's blocking the entrance to the hotel.

"Guess we're all spending the night here, huh?" the chef asked and cut some more bread for her.

"Good thing we have enough food," Line said.

The roof above them creaked. The chef looked up. A couple of drops of water fell down.

"What was that?" Line asked.

"Just an old hole in the roof that seems to appear every time we have a storm. Better get some buckets from out back to put under it if it's gonna rain all night. Tim and Robert come with me." The chef looked at her with a smile. "Be right back."

"I'm staying here with all this delicious food," she said and stuffed another piece of bread in her mouth, along with some foie gras.

Line had never tasted this delicious food before and was overwhelmed with how great it was. She wished she could eat it every day. Maybe it was one of those pregnancy cravings she had heard so much about. She liked the thought.

The door opened and someone came inside. Line used her fingers to get more foie gras in her mouth.

"Hey, chef, do you think you could ..." she turned on the barstool as she spoke, then stopped as she stared into the face of a wooden mask. "Wh ... who are you?"

If the person behind the mask smiled, Line wouldn't know since the mask covered the face so well she could hardly even see what color the eyes were.

"What do you want?" she asked with a shivering voice as she jumped down from the barstool with her heart racing in her chest.

Oh my God, Line. You have to run. It's him. It's the masked person who stuck a needle in Preben's eye!

Quickly, the masked person lifted a hand in the air and it was too late to react before Line realized it was holding a needle. She tried hard to fight the person away, but she was overpowered. Line screamed as the needle pierced through her right eye. She screamed and fell to the floor when the masked person finally let go of her. Shocked, she watched as the legs wearing black pants ran out of the kitchen and the door shut. Overwhelmed with anger, Line managed to get back up and follow after. She stormed out into The Yellow Room still screaming so loudly she didn't even hear that someone was screaming upstairs as well.

"Heeeeeelp!!" Line yelled.

She stormed out into the lobby, still screaming at the top of her lungs, then she fell to her knees in pain. She tried hard to see with her one good eye, only to realize that there was no one there. Only Preben who was lying on the mattress still whimpering in pain. Now he turned to look at her.

"HEEELP!" she cried. "Help me. It hurts!"

"They're ALL upstairs," he said. "Even the last bell-boy left a minute ago when we heard Emma scream from upstairs. It's just the two of us now. Scream all you like."

39

DECEMBER 2013

SOREN WAS HIDING. He still had the keycard and had used it to go through a big heavy fire door at the end of the hallway, closing it behind him, making sure Jacob couldn't follow him. The rooms in this wing had been hit by a tree and it was blocking the hallway, so he couldn't get any further. He had walked into one of the rooms where the tree had gone through the roof and found a closet he could hide in. It was freezing cold where he was and he was shivering. He found a blanket inside the closet and put it around him, but it didn't help much. The winds were strong and the rain was coming through the roof. The floors were soaked and the closet as well. Soren's shoes were wet and so were the bottom of his pants.

"Now what?" He asked in the darkness of the closet.

He could hear someone calling his name in the distance. It sounded like Emma. He wondered if she had come up there to look for him. Suddenly, he was afraid she would run into Jacob. Would Jacob hurt her? Would he kill her in his rage? Or would he tell her about how Soren stabbed him? Make them all think he was dangerous? Make them all think he was the one who had hurt Preben?

What's your plan? Wait for Jacob to find you? Way to paint yourself into a corner, once again. Why do you keep doing this to yourself?

Soren groaned. He knew Jacob would be looking for him and wouldn't stop till he had killed him. But Jacob was hurt, wasn't he? He was weakened by the stab in the back. Maybe, just maybe he would bleed to death or something before he found him?

If I stay here long enough.

But if he stayed there much longer, he might freeze to death. Or maybe the old house would fall on him and bury him alive. The roof above where he was hiding looked like it could cave in any moment. Soren had become very sober the moment he had struck Jacob with the knife. And now he felt the agony for the first time since lunch. The pain of what he had done and what was going to happen to him.

If he got out of there alive, he would still have to face Margit and the charges against him. He would rot in jail and maybe get killed on the inside. There was no way he would ever survive. Soren opened the door to the closet and walked out. What was the use of hiding anyway? No matter what he did, he was a dead man.

Might as well go out with a bang.

Soren stood in the center of the room while the storm raged above his head. He heard someone scream. It sounded like it came from the other side of the fire door. It sounded like a woman. Possibly Emma? A hope grew inside of him. Maybe she had found Jacob with the knife in his back?

Soren bit his lip. Would he dare to go back? Would he risk being found by Jacob who was probably lurking on the other side of the door, if he was still alive? Would he dare to stay and risk freezing to death or being hit by the falling roof or another tree? Oh what a mess it all was.

Soren looked around the room. Just a few hours ago it had been a nicely decorated hotel room. One of the nicer ones, he could tell. He sat down on the bed and threw a couple of branches on the floor along with a bunch of leaves. Then he stared at the small refrigerator in the corner. It was still intact and hadn't been hit by anything.

"Why the hell not?" he said out loud, got up from the bed and opened it. He found a couple of small bottles of champagne and pulled them out along with a chocolate bar and a white wine.

Might as well go out with a bang, right?

Soren popped the first bottle, put it to his mouth and drank insatiably. He was surprised to realize that he was able to empty the entire bottle without taking it away from his lips. He looked at the empty bottle while waiting for the buzz to kick in and make him forget his worries.

Yes, that was his plan. He did what he knew he was best at.

40

DECEMBER 2013

HE KNEW Soren was there somewhere. He couldn't just have vanished, Jacob thought to himself as he walked with heavy painful steps, grunting and groaning through the hallway as he neared the end of it. Jacob realized that Soren had the Master key and probably could be hiding anywhere by now, in any of the many rooms he knew Jacob couldn't enter since he didn't have a key.

Jacob reached the end of the hallway and realized it turned to the right a little and then stopped by an old iron fire door which had been set there in the building to separate the two parts of the hotel in case of a fire. With the door between them, they'd be able to prevent it from spreading from one wing to the other. He tried to open it, but it was locked. A small box with room for a card and a red light above it told him he needed some sort of key card to go through.

"Jacob? Soren?" The voice came from the other end of the hallway. Jacob walked back to the corner and looked around it. He spotted Emma walking with some guy knocking on doors. Jacob pulled his head back. He didn't want Emma to see him. Jacob was sweating now due to the pain in his back and he wondered if he should try to reach back there and pull the knife out.

Then he heard Emma scream. He jumped around the corner and sprang to her. He ran past the honeymoon room and wondered who had closed the door. He didn't give it much more thought as he continued towards Emma. She was lying on the floor with what looked like a body on top of her. The two bell-boys were both screaming too and tried to pull the dead body off of her.

"Let me," Jacob yelled as he grabbed the body's arm. The body slid off of her and landed on the floor with a thud. He turned him around and looked at the face.

"It's the clerk," Emma said gasping.

"It sure is," Jacob said without emotion. He examined the dead body and found marks from a string or something similar on the neck. "He was strangled with something," he said. "Could have been a cord. Or a very slim rope."

Emma gasped again and got to her feet. "Jacob?" she said and walked closer. "You ... you have a ... knife in your back?"

Jacob grunted. "Yes. Soren put that one in me. Don't think it hit anything vital though. It hurts like hell, but I can still move. I was lucky I guess."

"Soren? Is he the one? Did he do this to the clerk as well?"

Jacob nodded. He liked the idea of pinning everything on Soren. "I think he poked the needle in Preben's eye as well."

"But why? Why would he do such awful things?" Emma asked.

Jacob shrugged. It hurt like crazy but he tried to hide it from Emma.

"You're in pain, Jacob," she said. "Let's get downstairs and get some ice on your wound. Do you think it is best to leave the knife in? Or should we pull it out?"

Jacob could tell how appalled she was by the thought. It amused him. "So far the knife is helping to clot and stop the bleeding. Removing it would cause more damage to the surrounding tissue and nerves when we pull it out. Leave it in. They will remove it at the hospital."

He looked down the hallway again. "There is a door at the end of the hallway. I'm certain Soren is hiding on the other side. He has a Master key."

Emma looked at the dead clerk. "He might have one too."

"Good idea," Jacob said and started going through the clerk's many pockets. He found a keycard in the purple vest.

"Bingo," he said and pulled it out.

"So what do you want to do now?" Emma asked.

"You go down to the lobby and warn the others, then I'll try and get a hold of Soren. He can't have gone too far. We can't have him running around loose hurting more people."

Another scream suddenly filled the air and they both turned to look. "What was that?" Emma asked with a gasp. "It came from downstairs."

"I don't know. You go and find out. Take the bell-boys here with you and I'll pursue Soren," Jacob said.

"Be careful," Emma said before she left.

Oh I will.

41

DECEMBER 2013

I RAN DOWNSTAIRS AS FAST as I could with the bell-boys following me and my heart beating hard in my chest. I recognized the screams and knew they came from Line. I feared the worst as I jumped into the lobby and saw her. She was sitting on her knees on the tiles, her body bent forward in pain. She was screaming while blood was flushing out of her eye. Both Jon and Jesper stopped when they saw her, then turned their faces away.

I gasped and ran to her. "Line!" I kneeled next to her. "What happened?"

"Someone stabbed me in the eye," she cried.

"Where? In the bathroom?"

"No in the kitchen. I was in the kitchen ... oh my God ... it hurts so bad, Emma, do something; it hurts so much!"

"Who did this? Did you see who it was?"

"NO!" she cried. "He was wearing a mask of some sort. All I saw were his black pants as he ran away. Oh God it hurts. Please make it stop, Emma. Please make it stop. Do something, do anything."

I looked around desperately. I spotted a pack of painkillers next to Preben and picked them up. Preben suddenly sat up and grabbed my wrist.

"They're mine, "he said through gritted teeth.

I pulled my arm loose. "You can spare some for Line."

"No!" Preben said.

I ignored him like I ignored my children when they wouldn't share and walked to Line and gave her two tablets that she swallowed with some water I gave her. "I know it's not gonna remove the pain, but hopefully it can numb it slightly. I would offer you alcohol, but you can't drink it."

Jon and I carried her to the couch and helped her lay down while I fought my tears. It was horrible to see her like this and I couldn't stop my anger from growing. I was mad now, furious with Soren and I hoped Jacob would manage to find him. I couldn't believe Soren had gone rogue like this. I knew he had been acting crazy all day and drinking heavily so it kind of made sense, but it was still so hard to believe that he would do this to his old classmates. I could understand if he wanted to hurt Preben and Jacob, since they seemed like they had bad blood between them all day, but Line? And what about the clerk? What had he done to him? Maybe he had just been in his way. Maybe he discovered what he was up to.

But Soren was in the lobby with the rest of us when we heard the clerk scream. How could he have killed him and put him in the closet?

I looked worriedly at Line and hoped with all I had in me that her baby was alright. I put an ice-pack on her head to cool the areas around the eye down, then pulled out my phone once again to see if I had reception. I didn't, but I tried to dial 112 anyway, but it didn't go through. I tried to go online, but there was no Internet. I went to the counter and looked for a phone with a landline. I found one and tried to call, but it didn't work either. The winds were still blowing strongly outside and the wind howling through cracks in the old building. It was getting colder now and I was starting to freeze. Preben and Line were both moaning heavily. I couldn't believe this situation. It was such a mess. It made me so angry and, slowly, the anger pushed away my fear. I couldn't stop thinking about the secret host that the clerk was supposed to go and get, the same one who had invited us here, and who was supposed to be revealed to us at dinner. Who was it and why hadn't we seen him or her yet?

Could this host be working together with Soren on all this? If so, that meant that Jacob was in serious danger right now.

I looked at the stairs, then at Jon. "Do you have any weapons in this hotel?" I asked.

He shook his head with a whimper. He hadn't been able to take his eyes off of Line's eye ever since they had come back down. His entire body was shivering, his eyes wide and anxious.

Then it was like he remembered something. He looked at me. "Yes. Yes we do. We have hunting rifles for our guests who wish to go duck hunting on the plantation while they're here."

"Where? Where are they?"

"Locked in a cabinet in The Green Room. Down by the end wall."

"Who has the key?"

Jon shrugged.

"It doesn't matter," I said and stormed through the door leading into The Green Room. I found the cabinet next to the bar and grabbed the handle, but couldn't open it. I looked at the bar, spotted an icepick in a bucket and grabbed it. I slammed it against the glass in the cabinet, but didn't even make a crack. I swung it again against the glass, but it slipped and I hurt my hand badly and still didn't even scratch the glass.

I cursed and slammed my fist at the glass in anger, then took the icepick with me and ran back in the lobby.

"I'm going upstairs," I said and stormed past Jon. "You stay here and make sure nothing else happens to these two."

Jon looked frightened, then nodded.

"I'll be right back," I said and stormed up the stairs thinking only of Jacob and wondering if he was still alive.

"Jacob?" I called as I ran down the hallway with the blue carpet. "Jacob?"

I stopped in front of a double door with hand carved wood. It was closed, but something about it made me stop. I had a feeling, call it a hunch, but I knew I had to open it. I lifted my leg and kicked it till it opened.

Then I gasped. A set of eyes met me on the other side. They were familiar but belonged to a time long ago.

"Erik?"

42

DECEMBER 2013

HE HAD BEEN WAITING. Waiting and listening to what was going on downstairs, waiting for them to come and get him like they had planned to. The clerk was supposed to come and get him when dinner was on the table and everyone was sitting down. Erik was supposed to make a big entrance to the restaurant and hear everyone gasp. But something had gone terribly wrong. The storm had destroyed everything. When the clerk told him it was coming, he had at first thought it was a nice little effect, a gimmick to make the effect of his plan much stronger. But he hadn't thought of the consequences. He hadn't imagined how bad the events could turn. A tree had hit the wing close to his room and he had heard people scream like they were being killed. The clerk had never arrived and there had been so much turmoil in the hallway that he feared that everything had gone wrong somehow. Many times he thought they had succeeded in finding him. Especially when Jacob and Soren had crashed through the door and fallen into the living room of the suite. Erik had been in the bathroom when he heard the crash, but by the time he had maneuvered the wheelchair out of the bathroom, they were already running out the door. Erik had considered yelling something, but knew it wasn't the right time. He would only ruin the moment of surprise that he had planned for so long. So he had rolled to the door and closed it once they were gone, while wondering what the heck was going on with all of them. They were supposed to be in the restaurant now starting the first course.

Now he was looking directly at one of them who had kicked the door to his room in. She was standing in front of him with an icepick in her hand, panting, looking at him with suspicion.

"Erik?" she said.

Erik smiled. Then he spoke. "Keyboard. No. Cup."

Erik closed his eyes. This was so not how it was supposed to be. He knew he could do better. Years of training his brain had made it better, had made him better at controlling his speech, but stress and agitation always made his condition worse. This was not the time to panic. He could still surprise all of them.

"What?" Emma asked.

Erik shook his head. He tapped on his small computer that they had given him to communicate. The words he wrote were spoken out loudly by a mechanical voice.

"I'm sorry. I have trouble speaking," it said.

Emma looked confused. "Are you our host? I thought you were dead?"

Erik tapped on his keyboard. "Close the door, please."

Emma did so. Erik waited. Then he wrote. "Yes, I invited you all here. No I'm not dead."

"Why?"

"Why am I not dead?"

"No, why did you invite all of us here?"

"That I have yet to reveal. I'll do so when everyone is gathered at dinner."

"I think that might be hard to accomplish given the fact that two of your guests are seriously hurt downstairs and the other two are running around chasing each other. Did you plan this with Soren?" she asked.

Now it was Erik's turn to look confused. He tapped on the keyboard. "What are you talking about?"

"Soren has gone mad. He tried to kill Jacob. He stabbed him in the back. He stabbed a needle in the eyes of Line and Preben. Someone killed the clerk, but I'm pretty sure it wasn't Soren since he was with the rest of us downstairs when it happened. Were you in on it? Did you kill the clerk?"

Erik shook his head in bewilderment. He typed on his keyboard. The machine read his words out loud. "I have no idea what you're talking about. Do I look like I am able to kill anyone?"

Emma tilted her head slightly. "You've got a point. But then who did?"

Erik wanted to write something but he had no idea what. He was as confused as ever. While the roof above them creaked and another tree fell in the yard outside, he wondered if he had made a big mistake when deciding to gather all of them. Or was the unfortunate chain of events in fact an improvement on his original plan?

43

DECEMBER 2013

SOREN'S TEETH WERE CHATTERING. It was so cold in the room where he was hiding now and the winds outside were howling eerily. He looked at the small bottle of red wine in his hand and then down at the pile of small bottles he had taken from the mini-bar and emptied in the hope that the alcohol would keep him warm and maybe make him forget for a little while.

But none of those things had happened yet. He had a buzz going, but that was all. He still remembered everything and, worst of all, he still cared.

He heard someone moving behind the iron-door and froze. Then there was another sound like someone swiping a key-card and then the door slowly opened. Soren swallowed hard, then lifted the bottle and drank from it like had he been walking through a desert and this was his first bottle of water in days. He gulped it down desperately thinking it was probably going to be the last thing he did, when he heard Jacob's voice fill the air.

"Sooooreeen?" he called with an almost caring tone to his voice, like was he luring a cat or dog out from his hiding to go to the vet. "Where are you old boy? I'm coming to GET you!"

Soren drew in a deep breath, then emptied the bottle and threw it in the pile making a loud crash as the bottle broke. Jacob's face was soon in the doorway. He looked disappointed.

"You're not even trying to hide?" he asked.

Soren shook his head. He tried to get up, but realized he probably was a little drunker than first anticipated. He looked at Jacob with a blissful smile. Finally, the numbness had entered his body; finally, he didn't care anymore. Jacob could kill him if he wanted to. What did it matter?

"You do know I'm here to kill you, right?" Jacob asked.

Soren could tell Jacob was in deep pain when he tried to move his torso. Pearls of sweat sprang from his forehead. His cheeks flared and his eyes were glassy. Soren nodded.

"I think you might have a fever, Jacob," he said.

"To HELL with me," Jacob yelled.

"Suit yourself," Soren said, then looked at the top of the tree that had crashed through the roof and was now lying in the room. He wondered if the tree had felt anything when being deprived of its life here on this forsaken earth. He wondered if he would.

Jacob approached him. "Do you have ANY idea how much this HURTS?" he yelled as he pointed at the knife in his back.

"Not exactly, but I have a vague idea."

"It hurts like HELL!"

"I know."

"No you don't. No, you don't know," Jacob snorted pitifully.

It occurred to Soren that he was a little pathetic and he wondered what it was about him that he had always been so afraid of. Maybe it was simply his anger. Soren never liked it when people were angry. His dad had yelled at him a lot when he was a child and ever since then, he had always tried to please everyone. He just wanted them to be happy. That was why he always did what the other boys told him to in school. It had always left him feeling inferior and all of his life people had always treated him like he was a nobody. He had been trampled on for his whole life. Maybe that was why he enjoyed taking advantage of those girls in the ambulance so much. It gave him some of his manhood back.

Maybe he was just a pervert.

Jacob was very close to him now, standing in front of him and the bed where Soren was still sitting. He reached out his hands and grabbed Soren around the neck. Soren didn't try to escape his destiny. He turned his head to look up into Jacob's eyes while he felt his grip tightening and blocking his air. Soren gasped and felt his eyes widen. Jacob was groaning. Soren could see the veins pop out in his forehead and throat. Soren had never noticed before that he had a lot of acne.

Probably from the use of too many steroids.

Soren had seen it in patients before. When they collapsed at the gym and he had to take them in. As black spots appeared before his eyes, he wondered if Jacob had also developed *Gynecomastia*, man-breasts, like many others who had taken anabolic steroids for a long time.

A dizziness came over him and Soren closed his eyes to let the darkness finally take him. Just when he was about to say goodbye to this world and drift off into the unknown land of the dead, Soren was suddenly struck by a thought that made him open his eyes wide. With the last of his strength, he lifted his hand and poked his fingers into both of Jacob's eyes as hard as he could, causing him to stumble backwards and let go of Soren's neck.

Jacob held a hand to his eyes. "My eyes!" he yelled.

Soren coughed and fell to the floor as well while catching his breath. "I'm sorry," he managed to wheeze between coughs. "But I have to say something."

Jacob moaned.

"Come on," Soren said as soon as he had gotten his breath back. "It's not like I poked a needle into your eyes. It was just my fingers."

"It hurts like crazy," Jacob said.

"Well I had to do it. I have to tell you something. It's important."

Jacob shook his head while holding his hands over his eyes. "WHAT?" he yelled.

"I think you might be suffering from kidney failure," Soren said.

"What the ... What are you talking about?"

"You threw up earlier and had barely any appetite during lunch. Plus you're complaining about pain in your back."

"That's because I have a godddamn knife in it!"

"Okay, fair point, but am I right to assume that the pain isn't only concentrated on the upper part of your body but also in the lower part? Am I also right to assume that you had the pain before I stuck the knife in your back?"

Jacob went quiet. "Well ... yes. It started yesterday as a matter of fact."

Soren nodded. His neck was hurting. "I've seen it before. The use of anabolic steroids can cause this. Nine out of ten bodybuilders who use steroids develop a condition called *focal segmental glomerulosclerosis*, a type of scarring within the kidneys. It is a common cause of kidney failure for adults. It's very serious, Jacob. You need to go to the hospital as soon as possible."

"Wh ... what the hell are you talking about?" Jacob said and tried to remove his hands from his eyes. He blinked. "I was about to kill you, you little twit. You can talk all you want, but I'm not letting you go."

"You have high blood pressure," Jacob said. "You really shouldn't get too agitated. The kidney failure will cause you to be dehydrated and your heart might give out. I'd be very careful if I were you."

"Well, you're not me."

"Again you make a fair point ... but ..."

Jacob stood up and walked quickly towards Soren. Then he kicked him hard in the stomach. He lifted his fist high in the air and let it fall on Soren's face again and again. Soren tasted blood in his mouth and sank to the floor while Jacob continued the beating. Soren closed his eyes.

You deserve this, he told himself while taking the beating.

It wasn't until it suddenly stopped that he opened his eyes again. He looked up at Jacob who gasped for air with his eyes wide open, then fell backwards into the branches of the fallen tree with a loud crash.

44

DECEMBER 2013

"I THINK you need to come downstairs with me," I said.

I was still staring at Erik like I didn't quite believe he was actually there. "We all deserve an explanation."

Erik bit his lip. He rolled his wheel-chair back and forth on the carpet like he was speculating. He typed on the small computer he had in his lap. It spoke his words out.

"This is not at all what I had planned."

"Well maybe it's about time you let go of your plan. I mean there is no way you can pull it off now anyway, with all that has been going on."

I paused feeling a little tired of it all. I missed my family, I missed Morten and deeply regretted having taken off to come to this thing. Plus, it was getting late and I was starving, but who had the time to think about food? It was all a mess and I couldn't even call Morten for advice, even though I needed it more than ever. I had no idea how much longer those two downstairs could endure the amount of pain they were exposed to. I didn't know how much more I could endure. There was a dead body in the hallway that I had no idea what to do with.

"Okay," Erik's machine said. "Let's go downstairs, but I'll need your help to get down the stairs."

"Sure," I said and went to the double doors. I slammed them wide open. "After you."

Erik drew in a deep breath, then rolled towards me. "Here goes nothing."

I walked behind him pushing his chair down the hallway.

"So what was your plan anyway?" I asked. "To enter the restaurant during our dinner and reveal yourself and tell us all why you had us gathered, was that it?"

"Pretty much," Erik's machine said.

I bit my lip thinking I probably didn't need to tell him how ridiculous it all sounded. Like a bad movie or something.

Erik tapped on the keyboard. "Too lame?"

I laughed. "A little bit."

I looked at him sitting in the chair and started wondering what had happened to him. He used to be so handsome and athletic. Now his face was disfigured. "How did you end up in a wheelchair?" I asked.

He typed on the keyboard. "That was what I hoped this reunion could help me clarify."

"You mean to tell me someone here put you in that chair?"

"I believe so."

"That's terrible, Erik. Who?" I asked.

"I don't know exactly, but I have some ideas."

"Maybe it's all Soren," I mumbled. "He did try to kill Jacob, after all."

"He also killed Hans Frandsen. Hit him with his car."

I gasped and stopped pushing the chair. "What? How do you know that?"

"It doesn't matter."

"So what happened to you?" I asked and grabbed the handles of the chair again and started pushing. Further down the hall, I spotted the body of the clerk. Someone had covered him with a sheet, but a hand stuck out from underneath it. I shivered in disgust and focused my eyes on something else.

"I was hit by a car in 2005. I was paralyzed from the waist down and suffered brain damage."

"So this is all about revenge?" I asked.

Erik exhaled. He typed again, then deleted it. He wrote something else. "I just want answers."

I nodded. I could totally understand that. We came closer to the body and it was blocking the hallway, so I had to let go of Erik and move it to the side before I could maneuver the chair past the body. I grabbed the arm and pulled it while feeling like throwing up. Erik stared at it as we passed.

"The clerk?" the machine asked.

"Yes. Strangled with a cord or something. We think Soren did it somehow. He has been very drunk all day. Gone completely rogue."

"I see."

"I can't believe he's turned into this maniac. I mean, I know it's always the quiet ones, but come on. This is crazy if you ask me."

"You'd be surprised to know what secrets people hide."

"Yeah, but still ..." I was about to say something else when I was suddenly interrupted by a voice yelling from behind us. I turned to look.

"What the ...?"

I couldn't believe my eyes. Was that? Could it really be Soren? He was carrying someone in his arms. Was that Jacob?

45

DECEMBER 2013

"HELP ME."

Soren's arms were hurting under the heavy weight. He stared at Emma who looked like she had seen a troll.

"Please," he said. "I need help carrying him down the stairs."

Emma looked confused and a little frightened.

Soren moaned in distress. "Please," he said again.

Emma finally decided to step in and ran to him and grabbed Jacob's body from the other side just as Soren was about to drop him. She stared at Soren.

"Is he ...?"

"Dead? No. I gave him heart massage and mouth to mouth. He is breathing, but not conscious. I need to get him to a warmer place."

"Okay," Emma said, sounding like she didn't quite believe him. "What happened to him?"

"Heart failure."

"Okay. What happened to you? Your face is all beaten up," she said as they carried Jacob down the hallway.

"Jacob did it," he said. "Who's the guy in the wheelchair?"

"He'd probably like to tell you himself," Emma said.

They came closer and Soren saw his face. He gasped with surprise. Erik smiled.

"I ... I thought you were dead," he said. "I saw the obituary and everything."

Erik grinned. Soren recognized that smirk. Boy how he hated it. He waited for Erik to say something.

"Umbrella," he finally said, still with that smirk.

"What?" Soren asked.

Erik shook his head and clenched his fist. "Pillowcase." Then he blushed. Soren felt suddenly uncomfortable. This was very awkward.

"Maybe we should just keep moving," Emma said with a moan. "This guy is really heavy."

"Of course," Soren said.

"We have to lift him over Erik's head," she said.

"Naturally."

"On three," she said and started counting. "One, two ... and lift."

They both lifted Jacob into the air and carried him over Erik's head. Erik was typing on the small computer in his lap. A strange mechanical voice filled the air as they passed Erik and walked further down the hall.

"You'd like it if I was dead, wouldn't you?" the voice said behind them.

Soren turned his head and looked at Erik who was rolling his wheelchair after them with a clever grin.

"Just ignore him for now," Emma said. "We'll deal with all that later."

"Okay," he grunted. His arms were hurting badly. They were shaking with the strain and his body was aching from the beating he had received. But for the first time since they got there, he felt like he could actually accomplish something. He could do something right to make amends for all the wrong he had done. If he saved the life of the man he hated the most, then he thought it might somehow balance out all the bad. He had no idea if it worked like that, but he had to give it a try. He had to do what was right for once in his life.

Carefully they carried Jacob down the stairs where Line and Preben were still moaning and crying in pain in the lobby. They placed Jacob on the floor on a pile of pillows taken from all the chairs they could find nearby. It made a nice bed.

Jacob was pale when Soren kneeled next to him and felt his pulse. It was too fast. Jacob's heart was working too hard and that wasn't good. Soren looked at Emma who checked her phone once again to look for a signal when suddenly there was a loud crash outside and all the lights went off in the hotel.

46

DECEMBER 2013

"JUST WHAT WE NEEDED," I said. "A blackout."

"A fallen tree must have cut the power lines somehow," Soren said.

"What the heck is going on here? We need help!" Preben yelled while Line simply whimpered in fear and pain.

"I think we have a flashlight in the kitchen," The bell-boy Jesper said.

"We have candles in The Green Room," Jon said.

"Then go get them," I said.

"Okay," Jesper said.

Then I heard their steps and a door open.

"Hoopla?" It was Erik's voice from up the stairs.

"What was that?" Line asked.

"Erik," I said with a deep sigh. "Erik Gundtofte. It's a long story. I have to help him down the stairs."

"I thought Soren said he was dead," Preben wailed.

"Well he's not. He was hit by a car in 2005, but wasn't killed. He's in a wheelchair."

"Gonzo!" Erik burst out.

"What?" Line asked. "What did he just say?"

"Boobs."

"Excuse me?" Line said again.

"He's having trouble speaking," I said. "Don't mind him. He's just agitated because he wanted to reveal himself to you all during our dinner and now it is all spoiled."

"Is he the IDIOT who invited us here?" Preben yelled.

"Yes. He'll tell you everything himself," I said and fumbled my way towards the stairs.

"I'm gonna KILL him," Preben yelled. "Right after I kill you Soren for doing this to me!"

"What? I didn't do anything," Soren said.

"You stabbed Jacob," I said.

"Well yes. That I did, but not the other thing."

Erik was typing on his computer while I was deciding whether I believed Soren or not. Then the voice of the machine filled the air speaking some strange nonsense.

"I'm coming," I said realizing Erik probably couldn't see what he was typing and walked up the stairs feeling my way by the rail. Luckily the moon shone in the windows every now and then when it was free from a cloud and gave some light. I grabbed the handles of the wheelchair.

"Let me help you," Soren said and came up the stairs. He grabbed the wheelchair from underneath and helped me carry Erik down to the lobby.

"There you go," Soren said when we sat him down.

"Thank you," I said to him.

It was strange. I was both afraid of him and yet somehow felt like he was genuinely trying to help. Something didn't quite add up in my mind. I couldn't understand how he could have done this to the others and at the same time be trying to help. Either he was a psychopath of the worst kind or we were completely wrong about him. I couldn't figure out which explanation I believed the most.

Jesper returned with a lit flashlight.

"Where is Jon?" I asked.

"I don't know. I went to the kitchen to get the flashlight. The chef says they're done with dinner and have been for a long time in case anyone is hungry."

A silence spread across the lobby. I, for one, was starving, but didn't like to say it. After all, there were people in serious pain here. How could we eat?

"I'll get him to bring some food in here and then you can decide if you want any," Jesper said. He handed me the flashlight, then left again.

I started looking forward to getting something to eat when another bone-piercing scream made me forget all about food.

47

DECEMBER 2013

"WHAT WAS THAT?" Line cried.

"We'll have to go and check it out," I said. Then I paused. The screams continued. I wasn't sure I dared to go alone.

"I'll go with you," Soren said.

I put my hand in my pocket and felt the icepick that I still had on me. I clenched the handle between my fingers.

"Okay," I said.

"It sounded like it came from The Green Room," he said.

I lit the way as we walked. I wasn't sure I wanted to go into a dark room alone with Soren, but there was no way out of it. I grabbed the handle of the door, opened it and held the flashlight up in the direction of the screaming sound. The light fell on Jon, the bell-boy. He was squirming on the floor, while screaming in pain.

"My eye! My eye!"

We ran to him and I kneeled in front of him. "What happened?"

"I ... I was looking for some candles in the dresser right there. When I turned my head, someone was standing behind me wearing an ugly old mask. He ... He stabbed me in the eye with something. It hurts so badly!"

"A needle," I said, as I examined Jon's face. "Just like the others." I felt a chill run down my spine.

What if that person is still in here? What if he is watching us? Waiting to make his next move.

The thought made me paranoid and I turned with the flashlight to light up all corners of the room.

"Oh my God," Soren said.

I couldn't believe it. Now I didn't understand anything. Soren had been with me all the time, so it couldn't have been him. There was no way. It had to be someone else, but everyone else was hurt. Jacob wasn't even conscious.

Cross your heart and hope to die. Stick a needle in your eye.

Victor's words were flickering through my mind fast. I couldn't stop thinking about them. What was this all about? What the heck was going on here?

"Let's get him out into the lobby with the others," Soren said. "I think I'll see if I can go outside for help."

We helped Jon get up and carried him to the lobby.

"Don't," I said to Soren when we had placed Jon in a chair with no pillows. "It's too dangerous."

"I think it's the only way," Soren said. "People will end up dying in here if we don't get them to a hospital. They'll have to send a helicopter or something."

"Not in this weather." It was Erik's machine that spoke. I shone my flashlight on him.

Soren sighed. "Erik is right. They won't be able to get one airborne until the winds have ceased and that won't happen until early in the morning according to the weather forecast I saw on TV earlier in my room."

I tore at my hair in distress. This situation was unbelievable. "Then there really isn't much we can do, is there?" I asked. "We're stuck in here waiting to get our eyes poked out with a needle. I think I'll take my chances with the storm."

I walked to the door and looked out the window. Branches and trunks were airborne. If I walked out, I would definitely risk getting killed. I shone the flashlight at my old classmates in the lobby, then stopped when I found Erik.

"What the heck are we even doing here, Erik? Could you at least answer that before we all get killed?"

"Yeah I'd really like to know that as well," Preben said.

"Yeah," Line said.

"Yes, Erik, please explain," Soren said.

Erik exhaled. He opened his mouth to speak.

"Pillow," he said. "Paper, blade, pencil, knife."

"Use the machine," I said. "I'll light the keyboard for you so you can see."

Erik tapped. "Thanks," the machine said. "I was trying to tell you that I couldn't see anything."

48

DECEMBER 2013

EMMA WAS SHINING the flashlight in his face. It hurt his eyes. Erik squinted, then looked at his computer and typed the words he had been wanting to say for years and when planning this entire event. The computer voice read the words out loud. It made an echo in the lobby.

"In 2005, I was in an accident. I was hit by a car that left me paralyzed and with brain damage. I know whoever did this to me is present here today."

He looked up to see his classmates' responses. But none came. No gasps. No crying or pleading guilty. He was prepared for that. Erik typed again.

"Jacob threatened me shortly before the accident. Jacob, I believe you had a hand in this. I believe you put me in this chair."

Emma cleared her throat. "Jacob is unconscious," she said.

"Pocket!" Erik burst out unwillingly. He closed his eyes and tried to stay calm. If he got too agitated he couldn't stop words from jumping out of his mouth.

Don't lose control now. You've got them where you want them.

Erik opened his eyes again and typed. "Of course. I forgot. But to get to the bottom of this, I think Jacob arranged for me to be killed. I survived, but that wasn't his intention. I believe he and Preben had Soren hit me with a car."

"Leave me out of it," Preben said.

"Me too," Soren said.

Well this was highly annoying. The only one who could clarify this was unconscious. Now what should he do? Erik speculated. Nothing about this had turned out the way he wanted it too. Nothing about his life had turned out the way he wanted it to. It was all so ... so incredibly frustrating.

"Shellfish," he said.

Erik shook his head.

Keep calm. You can do it. You have to.

He typed again. The computer read his words. Oh how he loathed that female voice that had to speak for him. It always reminded him of the fact that he couldn't speak for himself anymore.

"So let me get this straight," Emma said. "You've invited all of us here and paid for our stay to find out who hit you with the car and maybe why they did it?"

Erik scoffed. He typed again. "No."

"Then why are we here?"

"I invited you all here for another reason." Erik sighed and rubbed his forehead. This was all wrong. Not at all the way he planned it.

"And what is that reason?" Emma asked. She seemed angry now. Her voice was trembling slightly.

"Spit it out you bastard!" Preben yelled.

Erik typed. He had to just tell them, didn't he? There was no way around it. "Well, as you might know, all who are present here share a horrible secret. One big secret that we had to carry for years and keep to ourselves."

The room went quiet. Even Preben stopped moaning.

"What secret is that?" Emma asked. She shone the flashlight in his eyes.

"Well Emma. You're the only one who doesn't know it, but it involves you. That's why you're here."

Emma grunted angrily. "What the ...?" She shone the flashlight at the others. Their eyes avoided hers. "What is he talking about? Preben? Line? Soren?"

"The content of the secret doesn't matter," Erik continued. "But I can tell you this much. No one in this room wants it to be revealed. We all swore not to. That's why we're here. That's why I invited all of you here."

"You're not telling her," Preben yelled. "I'm not tolerating it."

"Could anyone just tell me what is going on?" Emma continued.

"I'll kill you if you say anything," Preben continued.

Erik smiled. Maybe he could still get it the way he wanted it, after all. He typed again. "That's exactly what I thought."

"What do you mean?" Soren asked.

"Ever since I was put in this chair, my life has been miserable and not worth living. I have lost everything. My wife, my children, everything. I can't do anything, I can't even speak on my own. The last many years, I have been wondering how to get out of here and then I came up with this. By inviting you all here and threatening to reveal the secret we all share to Emma here, I thought I could manage to upset at least one of you enough to want to kill me. After all, you tried to kill me years ago, so now I'm gonna give you the chance to finish the job."

"What on earth are you talking about?" Preben asked.

"I want to be killed. I want to be put out of my misery. But I don't want to go unnoticed. I want it to be spectacular. So after much consideration, I found a way. I thought I'd do it like in the *Ten Little Indians*, you know the book, where someone invites all of them to the same deserted place. You haven't read it?"

"Can't say I have," Soren said.

"Nope," Line said.

"It's called *And Then There Were None*," Emma said. "The book is. The movie is called *Ten Little Indians*."

"Whatever," Erik's machine said.

There was silence in the room. Everyone was staring at Erik.

"Do you have any idea how insane all of this sounds?" Emma said.

"Yes, Erik," Preben said. "I can't believe you'd bring us into this situation just because *you feel bad about yourself.* I've lost my EYE here, Erik. Don't you think you're being just a little SELFISH? DON'T YOU?"

Erik nodded. Preben was getting himself all worked up. That was good. That had been Erik's intention all along.

"Yeah, why the heck did we have to get hurt?" Line asked.

Erik typed on his computer. "I had nothing to do with what happened to you. I'm very sorry that it did happen, but I had no part of it. I did not intend to hurt any of you; that was never my plan."

"How do you expect us to believe you?" Soren asked.

"Well, you just have to. Cause I didn't. I was here with you when the bell-boy was attacked, right?"

"He's got a point," Emma said.

"Thank you."

She shone the flashlight in his face again. "But that doesn't mean you couldn't have someone else here to do it for you."

Erik shrugged. Then he typed again. "Believe what you want. I'm sticking to my plan. If no one stops me, I'll reveal the secret tomorrow morning at breakfast. Now, if you don't mind, I'll roll into The Green Room and wait for my destiny."

Erik grabbed the wheels and started rolling towards the door. Emma shone the flashlight on it.

"How very theatrical," Preben yelled after him. "You always were such a drama queen."

Erik ignored him and kept rolling. He grabbed the handle and pulled the door wide open.

"Come on, Erik," Emma said. "This is ridiculous. You don't want to die. No one should die. We've had too much blood in this hotel already."

Erik turned around and looked at her even though he couldn't see her face behind the flashlight. He had dreamt about saying something so clever, something they'd all remember when they thought back on this weekend and his goodbye. His final words. He had thought about them for a long time and practiced them with his speech therapist, who had no idea why he wanted to learn these exact words, but never dared or cared enough to ask.

He opened his mouth and let the words glide over his lips just like he had rehearsed over and over again.

"Yippee ki-yay motherfuckers."

Then he smiled from ear to ear over his own victory, turned the wheelchair around and left.

49

DECEMBER 2013

I COULDN'T BELIEVE THIS. There was so much going through my mind at this exact moment. I was angry, sad, frustrated and afraid all at the same time. It was like a rollercoaster, really.

I stared at Erik as he left the room and suddenly remembered his tendency to overdramatize things immensely. It would have been funny and I would have laughed if the circumstances had been different. But they weren't. The situation was insane and I was certain that if I ever left the place alive no one would ever believe me. I wasn't even sure anyone would believe the story if I wrote it as fiction. It was simply too bizarre.

Meanwhile, the winds were howling outside the hotel and still making it impossible for us to leave or for the ambulance to arrive. All we could do was wait and hope to not be the next victim of the eye-poking psychopath who was running lose.

It was unbelievable.

And then there was this secret. It made me so angry that they all knew what it was, and that I was the only one who had no idea what they were talking about. It frightened me that it apparently was so gruesome a secret that they would kill each other to keep me from knowing it. What kind of secret is that bad if revealed?

The others in the lobby were all very quiet after Erik left. I couldn't see their faces, but the tension was thick. Preben and Line were still both in pain, but they weren't moaning as loudly as they had before. I guessed Erik had given them something to think about.

Something creaked and I shone the flashlight in the direction of the sound. It was Soren. He had gotten up from his chair.

"Where are you going?" I asked.

"I ..."

"Sit back down. No one is even going near The Green Room. I don't want anyone near Erik. I want to know this secret and if none of you present here will tell me, then I'll wait till the morning for Erik to spill the beans. I'm not leaving this hotel without knowing what it is. Just so you understand me correctly. The secret doesn't die with Erik either. No one kills him, do you hear me?"

Preben grumbled something and I shone the flashlight at him.

"That goes for you as well," I said. "We'll have no more killings, no more people getting needles in their eyes. This ends here. The bloodbath ends now."

The door opened to the lobby from The Yellow Room. I shone my flashlight at the door and spotted Jesper coming through it with a small wagon packed with plates and dishes.

"I brought food enough for everyone," he said with a wide smile.

"Jon was hurt," I said and pointed the flashlight on Jon. Jesper shrieked and ran to him. "I'm so sorry," he said to Jon. "Did you see who it was?"

"No," Jon whimpered. "It hurts so bad."

Jesper rose to his feet again and looked at me. "Guess no one is hungry anymore, huh?"

I shrugged. My stomach was growling. "I could go for a bite. Lord knows I need the strength to get through the night. Is there any coffee to help us stay awake?"

"No, but I can go back and get some," Jesper said. "I'm sure they have some in the kitchen. Let me ask the chef."

I grabbed his arm and held him back. "Don't. I don't like you running around the hotel all by yourself."

I took a piece of bread and found some foie gras that I smeared on it. It felt good to get something to eat. I found a soda, opened it and drank.

I shone the flashlight at the others. The entire scene reminded me of a lazaret from a war movie. Even Soren was so badly beat up that his entire face was swollen. But I no longer felt as sorry for them as I had earlier. Knowing that they were hiding something from me made me want to hurt them myself.

I decided to be the bigger person instead.

"Anyone else want something to eat?"

No one said anything. So I continued eating while keeping my flashlight on them, making sure none of them tried to make a move. I found a piece of cockerel breast in a sauce and ate it with my fingers. It tasted heavenly. Then I finished my orange soda, still keeping my eyes on the others. None of them spoke or even moved. I guessed they felt bad and I was happy that they did. I could maybe understand that the guys would do something horrible and keep it from me, but Line? She had been my friend. Was that why we lost contact after high-school? Was it because she couldn't face me?

I put the empty bottle down and suddenly another urgent need appeared. I tried to ignore it, but many hours of holding it in made it impossible to keep ignoring it. I looked at Jesper and handed him the flashlight.

"I need to go to the bathroom. I won't be long, I promise. All I need from you is for you to keep a close eye on everyone here. Make sure no one leaves the lobby. It's very important. If anyone tries anything, you come and get me. Knock on the bathroom door, okay?"

"Got it," Jesper said.

"Be right back."

50

DECEMBER 2013

I RAN TO THE BATHROOM. Literally. It annoyed me immensely that I had to go, but I knew I couldn't go all night without going, so now was as good a time as any.

I opened the door to the restroom, sat down and did what I had to do. Barely had I put back on my pants and washed my fingers before there was an eager knock on the door.

"Crap," I said and hurried to wipe my fingers on the towel. It had to be Jesper. Someone had tried something. "Be right there," I yelled and ran to the door. I grabbed the handle and swung the door open.

Then I gasped.

A mask stared back at me. A wooden African mask. The person wearing it was holding a flashlight in their hand that lit up the mask from underneath.

I backed up. "Wh ... Who are you?"

The masked person lifted their other arm and I spotted the long needle in their hand. Fear struck me. I screamed, then reached out both of my hands and just as the person struck the needle towards my eye, I pushed him in the stomach. The needle slid past my eye, but hit my nose instead and went straight through the skin.

I screamed as it pierced my nose. Then I reached down in my pocket and pulled out the icepick that I was still carrying around. The masked person was coming at me with fists clenched and took a swing at my face. With a roar, I swung the icepick and managed to hit their shoulder. The masked person screamed and fell backwards. I grabbed the handle of the icepick and pulled it out. The sound it made coming out of the shoulder was unbearable. With a grunt, I lifted the icepick again and stood bent over the masked person while holding it in the air. The masked person kicked me hard on the knee and I fell to the ground with a whimper. The person tried to get away, but I grabbed their leg with one hand, lifted the icepick with the other and hammered it through their thigh. The person screamed and whimpered. Once again I grabbed the handle of the icepick and pulled it out even though the sound almost made me throw up. I wasn't going to let go of my weapon and be completely defenseless. Like a crazy woman, I roared and stood with the blood smeared icepick above this mysterious person. Then, I reached down and grabbed the mask and pulled it off. A set of blue eyes looked back at me. I recognized them from somewhere, but couldn't quite figure out from where. They belonged to a woman about my age, with short blond hair. She growled, grabbed my hand and tried to bite me when I swung my fist through the air and hit her jaw. She was knocked back, but still awake as I grabbed her leg and started dragging her back towards the lobby. She screamed and tried to get loose, but I held her tight and she was in too much pain to succeed. I kicked open the door leading into the lobby and dragged her after me. A flashlight was pointed at me as I entered the room.

"Emma?" Soren said.

I grunted and pulled the woman across the tiles closer to the flock, then threw her on the floor. I took my belt and tied her hands behind her back.

"What on earth happened to your nose?" Soren asked.

I realized I still had the needle stuck in it and that it hurt like crazy. I lifted the mask into the air. Jesper lit it with his flashlight. A few people gasped. Preben yelled.

"That's it! That's the one!"

"I know," I said and looked down at the woman.

Jesper shone the flashlight on her face. Preben gasped. "I know you!"

"Chef?" Jesper exclaimed.

"No," said Preben.

"Yes," Line said. "That's the woman who gave me foie gras in the kitchen before I was attacked."

"But ..." Preben stopped.

"Maria?"

The voice was Jacob's. Jesper shone the flashlight on his face.

"Jacob?" I said surprised. I looked at him. He was sitting up but still looked sick, almost greenish in the face. He blinked and hid his eyes from the bright light.

"He woke up while you were gone," Soren said.

"You know this woman?" I asked Jacob.

Jacob opened his mouth but was interrupted before he could speak even a word.

"She is my wife." The sound of Erik's computer made me turn my head.

Jesper shone the light on him as he rolled his wheelchair through the door. "Sorry, couldn't help hearing the turmoil."

"Erik? She's your wife?" I asked.

"Was," he corrected me with the help of the computer. "We were divorced in 2009."

51

DECEMBER 2013

I STARED at Erik in disbelief. I felt confused beyond imagining.

"I have no idea what she is doing here," the computer said. "We split up four years ago and I haven't seen her or our children since. The mask I recognize, though. Maria traveled a lot before we met each other and was in Kenya in 1999 a few months before we met. It used to hang in our living room."

"Split up?" Maria hissed. "You threw me out. You threw all of us out, you heartless bastard. You turned your back on your own children."

"Yes, I threw you out. I didn't want to have you in my life anymore. Every time I looked at your face it reminded me of what had happened to me, of what I had lost. When I looked at you and the girls I remembered what I used to have and who I used to be. I didn't want to remember anymore. I wanted to forget, because I knew I could never be that person again or have that life anymore. Besides things had gotten out of hand in our marriage. I finally had enough, Maria. I wrote an e-mail to the police telling them you were keeping me hostage in my own house and that I wanted you out. Then I had my lawyer draw up the papers and soon the police came to remove you. You kept me locked up for years, Maria, while you partied and had sex with men near my door to make sure I could hear it."

"You were the one who pushed me away. With all the yelling and the cursing and calling me names. It was unbearable. Then you divorced me and left me with nothing. No money. A single mom with two kids and no job," she said. "I hadn't worked for years since I sacrificed everything, my entire career, so you could pursue yours, remember? Do you have any idea how hard it is to get a job when you've been out of the workforce for ten years? I used to be the head chef at Nimb, goddammit. At one of Denmark's finest restaurants. It has taken me the last four years to work my way back up again. I had to live with my parents for the entire first year. Do you have any idea how much of a torture that was?"

"Well boohoo for you," Erik's computer said. "At least you can still work. You can walk, you can talk to the girls and tell them how much you love them without having to have this mechanical voice speak for you. You can live like a normal person."

"Well tell that to the court that declared me to be an unfit mother and took the girls away from me, just because I had to spend six months in a mental institution."

"You tried to strangle your own mother, Maria."

"So you think it's better for the girls to be with that foster family that they're living with now, huh?"

"As a matter of fact, I do. Especially when I look at you now and what you've done. You have completely lost it, haven't you? You've gone mad."

"STOP!"

Jesper turned the flashlight towards Preben who was the one who had yelled. Still holding an icepack to his face, Preben had now gotten up from the mattress and was looking at Maria and Erik.

"Stop, stop, stop," he said. "I don't want to hear any more of your little quarrels. I want answers and I want them now. Why the HELL did I have to have a needle stuck in my eye, can you please answer that, huh, *dear* Maria?"

The flashlight was now on Maria's face. She grinned.

"Because you deserve it, you bastard. All of you. You ruined my life.

You destroyed it with that little experiment of yours, or game or whatever you call it. This was my way of getting back at you. If it hadn't been for you and what you did on your graduation night, I would still have my husband; I would still have my life."

"That's it," I said and stepped forward so Jesper could shine the light on me. "I want to know what she is talking about. Can someone please explain to me what she is talking about?"

There was silence for a long time.

"I think I deserve to know."

Then there was laughter. It was Maria who was laughing. "That's priceless. None of you have come clean yet, huh? Poor little Emma who doesn't know a thing."

"Don't tell her anything," Preben hissed.

"Why not?" Line suddenly asked.

"Because we all made a promise, remember? Emma could never know. You made an oath on your life," Preben answered.

"Yeah, but it kind of doesn't matter anymore, does it?" Soren asked. "

"What is that supposed to mean?" Preben asked.

"Erik already told us he will reveal everything to her in the morning if none of us kills him first."

"So what?" Preben said. "We just kill him, right? Jacob?"

"I don't know anymore, Preben. It has all gotten a little out of hand if you ask me. I mean, look at you and Line."

"I'll be glad to tell her," Maria said. "And, frankly, it doesn't matter if you want me to or not. I don't give a shit about any of you."

"Thank you," I said. I was still holding the icepick tight in my hand in case any of them tried anything. I wasn't so sure I could trust this Maria-person, she was grinning like a madman and had clearly lost it a long time ago.

52

DECEMBER 2013

"IT ALL HAPPENED at the graduation party," Maria said. "How much do you remember of that night?"

I thought for a few seconds. "Not much. Me, Line and three other girls had rented a limo to get to the party and drank loads of champagne on our way there. I was pretty drunk. I remember eating dinner in the big hall at the school and then dancing *Les Lanciers* as it is tradition. But that is pretty much it."

Maria smiled and tilted her head. "Well isn't that just *fantastic?*" She laughed. "So you don't remember Preben asking you to go to the dance with him?"

"Goddammit, Maria I'm gonna kill you," Preben yelled. "Did you tell her all this, Erik? Did you?"

"Yes," Erik said.

I blushed. "I don't remember that, no."

Maria laughed again. "Well then let me tell you everything. They made a race. All four of them were in on it."

"What kind of race?"

"A race to determine a bet they had made earlier in the evening. It was Erik, Preben, Jacob and Soren. In biology class, they had been discussing sperm with the teacher Hans Frandsen. Some new research that Jacob had come across suggested that female sperm traveled slower than male sperm. You know sperm can either be male or female, that is how the sex of the baby is determined. So the theory was that the male sperm was faster but didn't live as long and in their drunkenness that night the four boys decided to verify it. It started as just a joke while they were meeting at Jacob's house and having a few drinks before the party. After having smoked a joint and hit some speed, they started joking about it and suddenly one of them, Jacob again, I believe, told the others that they should make a bet. So they did. Jacob and Preben both put their money on the male sperm. They thought it was stronger and more durable than female, and that if you put those two up against each other, the male sperm would win; it would be a boy. Soren and Erik bet against them. They said the female could survive longer and endure more, so therefore, the female would win. At this point they were extremely drunk and arguing wildly. They were pretty out of it, so it never occurred to them that one or the other would always win ... that's how we end up with both boys and girls in this world. They were too drunk to realize that, of course, or this whole thing could have been avoided. They bet a lot of money and prepared the race. They decided they needed as much different sperm as possible to enhance the chances of having both female and male sperm in the sample and so they all masturbated into a cup and it was mixed into a needleless syringe. They brought Line into it, by asking for her help once they arrived at the party at the school. They told her they wanted to use you, Emma, and she had to lure you into the biology lab. Actually it was Preben's idea to use you, since he was so angry with you for refusing to go to the party with him, but anyway Jacob gave Line a Roofie, you know ... the drug and she slipped it to you in your drink at some point during the party at the school. Preben talked to you and hit on you until you passed out and he grabbed you in his arms. He carried you to the biology lab where they inseminated you with the semen from all four of them. They thought they were so clever and had so much fun with it. They made sure you got home alright and then went back to the school to party on like the animals they were. It wasn't until they sobered up the next day they all realized what they had done. But by then it was too late. You became pregnant, but they realized they could never tell you or anyone since they would end up in jail. So they swore each other to secrecy or death. Cross our hearts and hope to die, they said. So they kept this from you for all these years. There you go. That's the big secret that they're all willing to kill to keep, the one that destroyed my entire life. Jacob was so stupid and high that he took pictures of the entire thing with a camera that belonged to the biology lab. Hans Frandsen, the biology teacher saw the pictures and threatened to tell on them. Later, they had Soren kill him."

Maria stopped talking. An odd silence spread in the lobby. I stared at her not knowing what to say. I felt so many things that I had no words. It took me a long time to realize what this meant.

"Did ... is ... Excuse me ... what?" I stuttered.

In those minutes I was on a rollercoaster of emotions, but eventually the anger took over and make me clearheaded. My voice was quivering with anger as I spoke.

"So what you're saying is that one of these four bastards is the father of my oldest child? Is that what you're telling me here?"

Maria grinned. "I guess so. Big surprise, huh?"

"But ... but ... Is this some freaking joke? Preben? Soren? Erik? What is the meaning of all this? Line?"

"I ... I have no excuse, Emma," Line said. "You know I used to have a thing for Jacob ... I guess I thought if I helped them I'd ..."

"I don't want to hear it," I said. "I can't deal with your explanations right now. I need some time to think this ..."

I stopped myself. It suddenly all came together for me. It was true, my pregnancy with Maya had always been a mystery to me. I had become pregnant shortly after graduation, but I had always thought it was Michael who was the father. I had met him that summer only two weeks after graduation, and, by accident, I became pregnant. At least that was what I had thought, but the doctors kept telling me I was further along in my pregnancy than I thought. I never told Michael that since I thought it didn't matter. He was the only one I had slept with that summer, so it had to be him. We had Maya then split up for a couple of years when I dated someone else, until we finally got back together again and had Victor.

I fumbled backwards and found a chair. I sat down and held a hand to my face. It was like the entire foundation of my adult life had been pulled away from beneath me. How on Earth was I ever going to explain this to Maya?

53

DECEMBER 2013

"OKAY, so I buy the fact that you wanted to punish me and the boys for having destroyed your life," Line said to Maria. "But why did the bell-boy have to be hurt? Why did the clerk have to get killed?"

"The clerk was in my way," Maria said. "He was going up to get Erik and I had to prevent him from doing that. He saw me. He saw my face. So I strangled him. But he was expendable. The rest of you, I wanted to suffer like I had, not give you the pleasure of dying. I wanted you to look at yourselves in the mirror every day and be reminded of what you had done. The bell-boy was an accident. It was dark and I thought he was Soren. We can call it wastage, right?"

I felt sick from her cynicism.

"Why try and hurt me?" I asked, feeling the needle in my nose. It still hurt but I didn't dare pull it out. The mere thought of doing so made me feel even sicker. "I had nothing to do with any of it."

"Well, we're just the innocent little one, aren't we? To be honest, you're the one I'm mostly mad at. You deciding to have that baby ruined everything for me. Erik never stopped thinking about her and whether she could be his. That's why I had to stop him when he went to see you and tell you the truth in 2005. He was about to ruin everything. I couldn't have a husband in jail and a bastard running around demanding child support. It was humiliating. I had to prevent him from destroying my life."

"Even if it meant killing him?" I asked.

I looked at Erik who went pale. He typed on his computer. I saw tears roll across his face when Jesper lit up his face with the flashlight.

"You're sick, Maria. My God, how I hate you," the computer said. He hid his face in his hands and cried.

"That was why you called?" I asked him. "I remember you asked to meet me somewhere in Copenhagen at a park in 2005, but you never showed up."

Erik nodded and looked at me. He typed on his computer. "It had been torturing me for years. I wanted to tell you everything. I hated myself for what we had done. I still hate myself for it."

"But you never made it because ..." I paused and looked at Maria. She didn't even seem sorry for what she had done. "And all this time you thought Preben, Jacob and Soren did this to you to shut you up."

Erik nodded again. I could tell he wanted to say something, and it frustrated him like crazy that he couldn't. All these regrets, all this anger built up inside of him and he couldn't let it out properly. Instead, he cried. Hid his face and cried.

"You bastard," I said addressed to Maria. "You heartless creep."

The others went silent.

Jesper turned off the flashlight and told us it was to save battery, but in reality I think he had had enough. I think we all had. We just wanted it all to be over so we could leave this strange place and never have to see anyone in this room ever again. I kept wondering who could be the father of my child and kept seeing certain traits in her that reminded me of one of the four possible fathers. I had no idea what to do after this, how to handle this news, or if I should even tell her or Michael. It would change so much for her, but at the same time, she deserved to know. I kept thinking that maybe I could get to know who it was before I made my decision. If it was Jacob or Preben, I probably wouldn't tell her since it would only hurt her more, but either Erik or Soren could maybe make a decent father, if she decided to get to know her biological father. After all, Michael hadn't been there for her the last several years and he didn't seem like he wanted that to change, so maybe it would do her good to know there was someone else? But then again, it might also destroy too much for her. It would change so much in the way she looked at herself. And they were all creeps who had done a terrible thing to me. I wasn't exactly liking any of them very much right now.

I might have dozed off for a few minutes, but as I woke up, the lobby had become eerily silent as the storm seemed to have eased off outside and suddenly the lights came back on.

But as they did, I realized that both Maria and Preben were gone. All that was left on the floor where Maria had been was my black leather belt.

54

DECEMBER 2013

"I HEAR THE AMBULANCE!" It was Line who yelled. She got up, walked to the window, and looked out.

"It can't get past the fallen trees," she said. "Now they're getting out of the van and climbing over the trunks. They're coming!"

I felt relaxed, finally, but couldn't stop thinking about Preben and Maria. Where were they?

"Did anyone see where Maria and Preben went?" I asked.

Soren shook his head. "Who cares?" he said.

"They can kill each other for all I care," Line said. "I just want to get out of here. Oh my God, how I want to get out of here."

"Can't blame you," I said. "I still don't think they should be allowed to kill one another. I think Maria should have a proper trial and a sentence."

I still had the icepick, and I stuck my hand inside my pocket and felt it.

"Besides, Preben needs medical care and he needs to know the paramedics are on their way. I'll go and see if I can find them," I said.

"Do you have a death wish or something?" Soren asked. "I thought it was only in stupid horror movies that the women went off alone and got themselves killed. Let's keep it that way, shall we? I'll come with you."

"Okay," I said and walked towards The Green Room. Let's start in here."

Soren followed me through the door. It was getting lighter now outside as morning approached. I threw a glance around the room.

"No one here," I said. "Let's try next door in The Yellow Room."

I opened the door and walked through.

"It's hard to imagine that less than twenty four hours ago we were sitting in here eating all that delicious food, drinking good wine and thinking we were just here on vacation, huh? Boy, we were in for a surprise," Soren said.

"You can say that again."

"I guess that's life for you, huh? Filled with strange surprises," he continued.

"They don't all have to be bad," I said. "Let's look in the kitchen."

"It has been awhile since my life offered me any of the good ones, I can tell you that," he said with an awkward chuckle. "To be perfectly honest, I was planning on disappearing after this weekend. Drive to Spain and vanish, start a new life for myself or maybe just kill myself."

"It can't be that bad, can it?" I asked. "I mean you have a family who loves you and will be behind you on anything, don't you?"

"Not this time. I've done something terrible, Emma. Something I can't stay here and face."

I stopped in front of the door leading to the kitchen. "Running never solves anything, Soren. Just remember that."

Soren nodded. We entered the kitchen. "Preben?" I called. I heard a sound. "This way," I said and pulled Soren's shirt.

We reached the freezer room at the end of the kitchen. "It came from behind this door," I said and called: "Preben?"

I pulled the handle and it opened. Inside, I saw a sight I could have lived without seeing. From the ceiling hung Maria with meat hooks pierced through her hands, blood gushing down her arms. She was gagged with a cloth, naked, and very dead. As we came closer, I could tell she had been stabbed with a butcher's knife several times. Pieces of her skin were stripped off of her body the way a butcher cuts off meat from a cow. In the corner of the room, we found Preben. He was sitting with the knife in his hand, trembling and staring at Maria with one wide open eye. The eye with the needle in it was so swollen it was hard to tell it had once looked like the other one. I kneeled in front of him and grabbed the handle of the knife. I pulled it out of his hand and gave it to Soren.

"It's over now, Preben," I said and helped him get up. "You need to see a doctor now."

EPILOGUE

MORTEN CAME ALONG with the kids and my dad to pick me up at the train station in Esbjerg. I don't think I had ever been so happy to see anyone in my life and I threw myself into their arms and hugged them one after another like I had been away for years.

Especially Maya whom I held tight, then stared into her eyes for a long time. I removed some hair from her forehead and kept touching her face wondering if I could see any resemblance to any of the men who were her potential fathers.

"Take it easy, Mom," she said, annoyed. "It's getting a little creepy. Jeez. You've only been gone for two days."

"I know," I said with tears in my voice. "But it seems like you've grown so much while I was gone. You're this little adult all of a sudden. I can't seem to get used to that."

Maya responded with a deep sigh.

"Let me take your bag," Morten said and he pulled it out of my hand. Our eyes locked for a second and I saw the worry in his. After the paramedics arrived and took care of all of us, the police came to take our statements and take in Preben for the murder of Maria. As soon as I had reception back, I called Morten and told him everything. Crying and sulking like a little girl, I told him everything that had happened at the hotel and all about Maya and what they had done to me back then. I told him to never tell anyone. Especially not Maya. I wasn't prepared to tell her anything yet.

"Cross my heart and hope to die," he said.

I told him to never say that again, either.

Now, he kissed me on the cheek and we started walking towards the car. I looked at Victor who, for once, looked back at me through the bangs that were always covering most of his face. The way he looked at me made me feel like he knew everything, but with him, you could never know for sure.

"Mom what happened to your nose?" Maya asked.

I reached up and felt the band aid the nurse had put on when they pulled the needle out. The needle had gone through and would leave a scar on both sides, the doctor at the hospital had told me. But it had done no damage to anything important, so I didn't need to worry. It was all cosmetic. I didn't mind too much. At least I still had both my eyes. That was more than I could say for Line, Preben and Jon. Theirs couldn't be saved and they had to get by with just the one from now on. I felt bad for them for having to live with this for the rest of their lives, but I was just glad I never had to see them again. Soren had taken off as soon as the police arrived. He didn't say goodbye, but I spotted him running out the back door with his suitcase in his hand and my guess was I wasn't going to see him ever again. Erik was the only one I said goodbye to and I told him that I wasn't ready to forgive just yet, but at some point I might be able to. I told him when that time came I would like for him to take a paternity test to see if he was the father. I couldn't promise him when it would be, since I needed some time to think this through. But I promised him I'd be in touch.

"I don't deserve it," he had said.

"No one deserves to be a parent," I answered. "But if they are, they deserve to know. So does the child."

I looked at Maya as we walked. She wrinkled her nose at me.

"It looks like you tried to pierce it yourself or something," she continued.

"Well that isn't too far from the truth, sweetheart," I answered.

"That is so lame, Mom. Really. So embarrassing."

The End

———

Want to know what happens next? Get the next novel in the Emma Frost Mystery series, <u>Peek a Boo, I See You</u>

AFTERWORD

Dear Reader,

Thank you for purchasing *Cross Your Heart and Hope to Die*. It is the fourth book in my Emma Frost series; so if you haven't read the three previous novels, then get them by following the links on the next pages.

Could I please ask you to leave a review on Amazon? That would mean the world to me. If you enjoyed this book, then maybe you'd enjoy my other mystery/horror series as well. It's called the Rebekka Franck Series. Just follow the links below to get them.

Maybe you enjoy the horror parts of this book. If so, then you might like some of my horror-stories from Denmark. On the following pages you can read an excerpt from the collection of horror stories that I have written called *Horror Stories from Denmark*.

Take care,
   Willow

Tired of too many emails? Text the word: "willowrose" to 31996 to sign up to Willow's VIP text List to get a text alert with news about New Releases, Giveaways, Bargains and Free books from Willow.

ABOUT THE AUTHOR

The Queen of Scream aka Willow Rose is a #1 Amazon Best-selling Author and an Amazon ALL-star Author of more than 80 novels.

She writes Mystery, Paranormal, Romance, Suspense, Horror, Supernatural thrillers, and Fantasy.

Willow's books are fast-paced, nail-biting page-turners with twists you won't see coming.

Several of her books have reached the Kindle top 20 of ALL books in the US, UK, and Canada.

She has sold more than four million books all over the world.

Willow lives on Florida's Space Coast with her husband and two daughters. When she is not writing or reading, you will find her surfing and watch the dolphins play in the waves of the Atlantic Ocean.

———

To be the first to hear about new releases and bargains— from Willow Rose—sign up below to be on the VIP List. (I promise not to share your email with anyone else, and I won't clutter your inbox.)

- Go here to sign up to be on the VIP LIST :
http://bit.ly/VIP-subscribe

Tired of too many emails? Text the word: "willowrose" to 31996 to sign up to Willow's VIP text List to get a text alert with news about New Releases, Giveaways, Bargains and Free books from Willow.

Cover design by Juan Villar Padron,
https://juanjjpadron.wixsite.com/juanpadron

Special thanks to my editor Janell Parque
http://janellparque.blogspot.com/

———

To be the first to hear about new releases and bargains from Willow Rose, sign up below to be on the VIP List. (I promise not to share your email with anyone else, and I won't clutter your inbox.)

- Tap here to sign up to be on the VIP LIST -

Tired of too many emails? Text the word: "willowrose" to 31996 to sign up to Willow's VIP text List to get a text alert with news about New Releases, Giveaways, Bargains and Free books from Willow.

Follow Willow Rose on BookBub:

Connect with Willow online:
Facebook
Twitter
GoodReads
willow-rose.net
madamewillowrose@gmail.com

CPSIA information can be obtained
at www.ICGtesting.com
Printed in the USA
LVHW030047220121
677169LV00039B/1098/J